DEADLY BITES ON WINTER NIGHTS

AN IVY CREEK COZY MYSTERY

RUTH BAKER

CLEANTALES PUBLISHING

Copyright © CleanTales Publishing

First published in December 2022

All characters and events in this publication, other than those clearly in the public domain, are fictitious and any resemblance to real persons, living or dead, is purely coincidental.

Copyright © CleanTales Publishing

The moral right of the author has been asserted.

All rights reserved. This book or any portion thereof may not be reproduced or used in any manner whatsoever without the express written permission of the publisher except for the use of brief quotations in a book review.

For questions and comments about this book, please contact
info@cleantales.com

ISBN: 9798367087109
Imprint: Independently Published

OTHER BOOKS IN THE IVY CREEK SERIES

Which Pie Goes with Murder?

Twinkle, Twinkle, Deadly Sprinkles

Eat Once, Die Twice

Silent Night, Unholy Bites

Waffles and Scuffles

Cookie Dough and Bruised Egos

A Sticky Toffee Catastrophe

Dough Shall Not Murder

Deadly Bites on Winter Nights

A Juicy Steak Tragedy

AN IVY CREEK COZY MYSTERY

BOOK NINE

1

"Did you hear the weather report?" Betsy asked, her eyes merry, as she came bustling through the front door of Sweet Delights Bakery. "They say we might get snow this weekend!"

Lucy couldn't help but smile, glancing over from her task of writing specials on the bakery chalkboard. Betsy was her youngest employee, in her early twenties, and her enthusiasm was infectious.

Hannah Curry groaned theatrically, setting down her tray of freshly baked turnovers. As Lucy's star baker, she'd had to prepare double the usual amount of pastries this morning. The chilly December mornings seemed to have whet the appetite of Ivy Creek's citizens.

"Not more snow," Hannah complained, though her lips twitched with humor. "We still have snow on the ground from last week."

Betsy wrinkled her nose as she tied on her apron. "Only an inch or two, and it's dirty."

Aunt Tricia added her two cents, not looking up as she stocked the cash register for the day. "It would be nice to have a fresh blanket of snow on the ground for Christmas."

She finished and turned to regard Lucy. "When are you and Taylor planning to pick out a tree for our house?"

Taylor Baker was Ivy Creek's deputy sheriff, and Lucy's beau. He was a frequent dinner guest at Lucy and Aunt Tricia's house; the home that Lucy had grown up in. Lucy's parents had tragically passed away less than two years ago, prompting Lucy to move back from the city where she'd worked as a food blogger. She'd taken over the family's bakery business with some misgivings at first, but now she couldn't imagine doing anything else.

"We were hoping to go one day this week," Lucy answered, as she carefully printed the new holiday coffee flavors in chalk. "I'll be buying a few wreaths as well, at least one for here, and one for the house. Nelson Farm has such a great selection!"

"Oooh, you're going to Nelson Farm? I want to go!" Betsy called out. She'd gotten right to work, wiping down the glass on top of the pastry case. "And Joseph will, too, of course. We're going to decorate a tree at his house." She sighed happily. "This will be our first Christmas together." Betsy was dating Joseph Hiller, the town's theater director, and was thoroughly smitten.

"Count me in, too," added Hannah. "I'm not sure about a tree, because Spooky might climb it. But I need a holiday wreath."

Lucy grinned at the mention of Spooky, Hannah's new cat. The stray had shown up at the bakery in October, and Hannah had promptly adopted her.

"OK, that sounds like fun!" Lucy said. "A group outing. Aunt Tricia, do you want to come with us?"

Aunt Tricia waved a hand. "As much as I like the *look of winter* - through the window of a warm house - I'm not too fond of tromping around outside this time of year. I'll pass, dear."

Lucy nodded. "OK. I'll talk to Taylor tonight and let you guys know when. Thankfully, things have been pretty calm in town lately, and he's been able to work regular hours."

She suppressed a shudder, thinking of last October, when Taylor had worked around the clock to solve the murder at the Haunted Forest attraction, where one of the actors had become a victim. During the investigation, Lucy had unknowingly put herself on the killer's radar, and she and Hannah had barely escaped with their lives.

Hannah surveyed the full pastry case, hands on her hips. "That ought to do it, for the morning rush, anyway," she commented. Turning to Lucy, she asked, "What's next?"

Lucy tapped her chin thoughtfully for a moment. "Fruitcake," she decided. "I dug out Mom's old recipe and made a few tweaks. I think we should start with ten cakes and go from there."

Hannah gave a mock salute and headed back into the kitchen. Lucy glanced around the bakery, which seemed bare now that they'd taken down the Thanksgiving decorations.

"Betsy," she began, knowing this was a task the young woman would love. "There's a box in the office marked Christmas decorations. Could you run upstairs and grab it, please? I think we should start with hanging the snowflakes."

Betsy's face was wreathed in smiles as she nodded, hurrying away. Aunt Tricia poured herself a peppermint mocha and tilted her head, regarding Lucy with a speculative gleam in her eye.

Lucy raised her brows. She knew that look. Aunt Tricia was scheming.

"What?" she finally asked, unable to guess what was on her aunt's mind.

Aunt Tricia just smiled and shook her head slightly. She sipped her coffee for a moment before she spoke.

"I was just thinking of your parents," she replied, nostalgia softening her features. "They got engaged at Christmas, you know."

Lucy nodded. "Yes. I know." She'd heard the story many times.

Aunt Tricia's lips curved. "Christmas is such a nice time to make a lifelong commitment..." She let the words trail off.

Lucy laughed. "Auntie!" She shook her head with amusement and turned away.

Her aunt was always dropping hints that she and Taylor should get married. It was true; they had known each other forever. They'd been high school sweethearts, but Lucy had broken Taylor's heart when she'd decided to stay in the city after college.

She'd been so young then. She'd wanted to see what the world had to offer outside of Ivy Creek. It had been very awkward between them when she'd moved back, but gradually they'd become good friends. Just recently, they'd both admitted the spark of attraction had never faded, and so began dating exclusively again.

But she and Taylor were happy now, just the way they were. *Why change that?*

The bakery's bell jangled as a customer entered, and Lucy looked up from her musings.

It was Lenora Nelson, the matriarch of Nelson Farm. Lucy smiled in welcome, and Aunt Tricia stepped forward to embrace her old friend.

Nelson Farm had been an Ivy Creek landmark for as far back as Lucy could remember. As a child, her father had always taken Lucy along to go pick out their Christmas tree – a special outing for just the two of them. And as a family, they'd always bought their fall apple cider and Halloween pumpkins there, too.

"Lenora!" Aunt Tricia stepped back and smiled fondly at the other woman. "How are you, dear?"

"Hi, Mrs. Nelson," Lucy said, with a warm smile. "We were just talking about coming out to the farm for our tree."

She couldn't help but notice the older woman's expression seemed strained, despite the smile she offered. There were lines of weariness on her face that seemed new, and her dark hair seemed greyer than when Lucy had seen her, just two months before.

"Hello, my friends," Lenora greeted them with forced cheer. "They say we might get some snow." It was a transparent attempt at optimism, which fell flat.

Aunt Tricia wasn't fooled by her friend's light tone. "Lenora, what's happened?" She searched the other woman's dark eyes.

Lenora seemed to deflate, her shoulders sagging, and Lucy suggested, "Let's sit down."

She steered the woman to a corner table, and Aunt Tricia settled across from her.

Lucy crossed the bakery to quickly pour a coffee for Lenora, black, as she knew the woman preferred it. She hurried back, pressing the cup into the woman's chilled hands, and pulled up a chair for herself.

Lenora stared down at the cup in her hands for a long moment, turning it round and round, before looking up into their worried faces.

"I'm afraid I have some bad news," she began, her eyes full of sorrow. She took a small sip of coffee to bolster herself before continuing, her voice grim.

"This will be our last Christmas. I'm out of options. I must sell Nelson Farm."

2

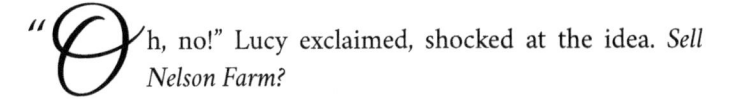

"Oh, no!" Lucy exclaimed, shocked at the idea. *Sell Nelson Farm?*

"Good heavens, why?" asked Aunt Tricia, her face showing her dismay.

Lenora sighed, a long and weary breath, before shaking her head sadly.

"We've been skating on thin ice for a while," she admitted. "Some... family problems," she hedged, and Lucy frowned. The older woman continued, despair coloring her voice.

"I was counting on August's harvest to pull us through. Jonas tried so hard this year, planting ten additional acres of corn to sell to the feed store. He put in the effort of two men." Pride in her youngest son was evident in Lenora's tone, and Lucy nodded encouragingly.

Jonas Nelson had been quite rowdy growing up, with some minor brushes with the law in his late teens. Lucy knew he was a good man at heart. It had just taken some time for him to mature. She suspected his fiancé, Heather Kelly, had a hand in turning Jonas around. He had proposed to Heather just last year. Lucy was already dreaming up ideas for their wedding cake, though they'd not yet announced a date.

"Jonas has turned into a fine young man," Aunt Tricia commented, approvingly. "But what went wrong?"

Lenora's expression turned dark. "That neighbor of ours, Chad Prentiss, and his new leather tannery. As soon as he began production there, our crops started to fail. We lost about 90% of our corn. Jonas suspects he's been dumping his factory wastewater directly into the river upstream from us."

Lucy was appalled. "Have you reported it to the EPA?"

Lenora shook her head, her expression grim. "We don't have proof yet. Jonas went to have a talk with Prentiss, and they wound up in an argument, with the man ordering him off the property. Jonas has since taken a sample of the water and sent it to be tested."

"Oh, my," murmured Aunt Tricia. "Even if it comes back showing pollutants, the damage has already been done."

"Exactly," sighed Lenora, her face weary. "Although, as my son told the man, if we find proof, we'll be taking him to court! But even if we're awarded compensation for our loss, it may be too late to save the farm."

Aunt Tricia squeezed her friend's hand. "Lenora, let us help."

Lucy chimed in. "Yes, please, Mrs. Nelson. We have a little extra."

Lenora smiled softly, but shook her head. "Thank you, my friends, but I can't accept your money." She held up a hand to stop their protests. "No, no. But there is one thing you may be able to help me with."

"Whatever you need," Aunt Tricia said, and Lucy nodded her agreement.

Lenora said, "This won't save the farm, but it could buy us some time." She paused. "As you probably know, I can be pretty handy in the kitchen…" This was said with a small smile. Nelson Farm often featured an assortment of baked goods during the winter months.

Lucy opened her mouth, ready to offer employment, but Lenora stopped her, knowing what she was thinking. "Oh, I'm not asking for a job. I'm still needed on the farm. But I've been thinking about selling my homemade dog biscuits here in town. Our dog, Ivan, adores them! And with Christmas coming, I think there might be a market for dog cookies."

She looked around the bakery's front room with admiration. "I would love to have a small vendor space here, if you had room."

"Absolutely!" Aunt Tricia beamed, pleased they could be of help.

"That sounds like a great idea!" Lucy exclaimed. "We have plenty of room."

Lenora smiled, rising from the table. "Thank you so much, my dears. I'll come back in a few days with a big batch of dog biscuits, all packaged and priced."

She and Aunt Tricia exchanged a quick hug, and Lenora took her leave, letting in a chilly blast of air through the door.

Lucy and Aunt Tricia looked at each other silently, both thinking the same thing.

Ivy Creek just wouldn't be the same without Nelson Farm.

"Brrr..." Lucy shivered and stamped her feet as she unlocked her front door. The temperature had dropped at least fifteen degrees in the last hour, and it was just after dusk.

Lucy had taken the long way home, driving through town, looking for an inspiration as to what to buy Aunt Tricia for Christmas.

The problem was, Aunt Tricia seemed to have everything she needed. She wasn't the type to want new gadgets or clothes. She was satisfied with the heirloom jewelry she'd acquired over her lifetime, and not enamored of modern styles.

She loved her books, but she tended to buy books on a whim, immediately upon desiring them. So much so, that Lucy couldn't think of a single book that Aunt Tricia would like that she didn't already own.

In short, Lucy was stumped. And Christmas was only weeks away.

Her meandering route through town hadn't yielded any ideas, so she'd headed home, deciding to pick Hannah's brain the next day. Maybe Hannah would have a fresh take on her dilemma.

Lucy stepped over the threshold, shutting out the cold behind her. The warm and cozy interior was welcome on her frozen face, and she sighed contentedly. It was good to be home.

"Aunt Tricia? I'm home!" she called out, crossing to the closet and removing her coat.

Gigi trotted into the living room and rubbed against her leg, purring.

"Hey there, little girl," Lucy said, reaching down to pet her white Persian. "You're lucky to be inside on a night like this."

She walked into the kitchen with Gigi at her heels. "Auntie?"

Gigi reached up and tapped Lucy on the leg, reminding her she hadn't been given a treat yet. Lucy chuckled and opened the cabinet, retrieving the treat pouch. As she opened the package, she heard her name being called from somewhere else in the house. It was Aunt Tricia, but she sounded far away. *Was she in the attic?*

She dropped the cat treat into Gigi's dish and set off to find her aunt, wandering down the hallway.

The stairs that led to the attic had been dropped down and unfolded, and Lucy grinned, peering up through the opening. Aunt Tricia must have been inspired by Betsy decorating for Christmas today. The Christmas decorations they stored upstairs were the only reason Aunt Tricia would ever venture into the attic. Her aunt had a phobia about bats and spiders.

"Auntie?" Lucy called and heard a muffled response.

She began climbing the steps carefully, calling, "You should have waited for me to come home. I would have brought the boxes down."

Just as she finished speaking, there was a crash, like the shattering of glass, followed by Aunt Tricia's loud cry of dismay.

Lucy ran the rest of the way up the stairs, her heart racing.

3

"Auntie, what happened? Are you alright?"

Aunt Tricia appeared to be physically fine, standing over a box on the floor, though her hands were pressed to her mouth. Lucy breathed a sigh of relief that her aunt hadn't fallen.

The older woman's face filled with sorrow as she crouched to examine the box's contents. Lucy moved to bend beside her, and the reason for Aunt Tricia's distress became clear.

Her aunt's most prized Christmas decoration, a twenty-two-inch Atlantic mold ceramic tree, lay shattered inside the box. Lucy's heart sank.

"Oh, Auntie! I'm so sorry! Do you think we can glue it?" The ceramic tree had been a gift from Lucy's uncle, long since deceased. She knew how much it meant to Aunt Tricia.

Her aunt was silent for a moment, reaching into the box to pick up a few pieces. She sighed and shook her head. "I'm afraid not. There are too many pieces, and the paint has chipped from the impact. It would never look right again. Oh, how could I have been so clumsy?"

Aunt Tricia sighed again and stood up, and Lucy stood with her, laying a hand on the woman's arm.

"Maybe we could buy a new one?" She knew it wouldn't be the same, but her aunt looked so sad. Lucy wanted more than anything to rewind the day, so she could have taken the box down herself.

Aunt Tricia smiled sadly. "They stopped making these a long time ago, dear." She brushed her hands together, trying to rid herself of her melancholy. "Well… what will be, will be. Let's see what else we have up here."

Lucy glanced once more inside the box before joining Aunt Tricia to survey the stack of cartons under the eaves. Together, they dragged the three remaining boxes labeled "Christmas" over to the attic opening.

"Let me get them," Lucy insisted, climbing a few steps down and reaching up. Aunt Tricia passed her the cartons, and one by one, Lucy brought them into the living room, returning to the stairway to supervise Aunt Tricia on her descent.

They closed the attic stairs with Lucy resolving to find a downstairs storage place for the boxes from now on.

"It's a bit late tonight, to start decorating," Aunt Tricia commented. "But I wanted us to have these ready for when you and Taylor bring home the tree."

Lucy agreed. It was getting late in the evening. Better to start fresh on a new day.

They passed the evening companionably in the living room, with Aunt Tricia ensconced in a book while Lucy and Gigi snuggled, watching a movie.

It was only later that night, as Lucy hopped into bed, that she realized that she now had an idea for Aunt Tricia's present: an Atlantic mold ceramic Christmas tree. If she were able to find one in time…

It would never be the same as the one her uncle had given Auntie, but maybe it would ease her sorrow.

Lucy looked up as the bakery bell jangled, pleased to see her neighbor, Donna Yeats, come through the door. The woman was all bundled up in a red knit hat and matching mittens and scarf, and her nose was pink from the cold.

"Hi, Donna! How are you?" Lucy asked. "Are you guys all ready for Christmas?"

"As ready as I'll ever be!" Donna said with a laugh. "I swear, every year it seems like less time between Thanksgiving and Christmas."

Lucy chuckled. "Yes, I've often thought those two holidays could be spaced out a bit more."

Donna removed her mittens, stuffing them in her pocket. "I'm here on a mission, Lucy. Chelsea will be in the Christmas Choral Concert this year, and I thought it would be nice to have cupcakes for all the kids for their rehearsal the night before."

Lucy smiled. "That's a great idea! When's the concert? I'd love to go, and I'm sure Taylor and Aunt Tricia would, too."

Donna beamed. "The concert is on the 23rd. That would be so lovely, if you guys could make it. Chelsea has a solo in Silent Night, so we're very excited." Her voice was full of pride.

"Oh, how wonderful! Yes, we'll definitely come. Now, what flavor cupcakes were you thinking? Or maybe do a mix?" Lucy asked, pen poised.

The ladies conferred on the details, and a few minutes later, Donna was pulling on her mittens and waving goodbye from the door. The bell jangled as she let herself out.

Lucy hummed to herself as she filed the order. *There was nothing like a choir of children singing Christmas carols to get you in the holiday spirit.*

Hannah came through the archway from the kitchen, her arms laden with several packaged fruitcakes.

"Where should I set these?" she asked, looking for an empty spot.

Lucy made room on top of the glass case and Hannah set the cakes down with a sigh. "I've taken five orders for fruitcake just this morning," she announced. "These are the last ones that aren't spoken for."

Lucy grinned. "That's what I like to hear! I'll come into the back and help you whip up another batch."

Aunt Tricia was just descending the stairs that led to the office and veranda area, which was closed for the winter season. "Did I hear you say you've almost sold out of fruitcake? I promised Mrs. Lovell two, for pick up tomorrow."

Hannah replied, "OK, I'm on it." She turned to Lucy. "I think your new recipe is a hit! We should start making them in bigger batches." She eyed the lobby space. "If we can find room for them."

Lucy nodded thoughtfully. "You know, maybe we should think about supplying one of the supermarkets. That way, we can make big batches without them taking up storage space here."

Aunt Tricia nodded. "That's a smart idea, Lucy. You could put some of those cute logo labels on them that we used for the summer fair." Sweet Delights' logo was done up in their trademark colors of pink and black, and Lucy adored it.

Lucy nodded absently, already crunching numbers in her head. She arrived at a price that would be appealing to a large store and still make a decent profit for the bakery. She pondered the notion a few heartbeats more. *Well, what would it hurt? Christmas season would be over in a matter of weeks. Might as well give it a try.*

"I'll be in my office for a few minutes," she called out, heading for the stairs.

A few minutes later, she was on the phone with Danny Bing, owner of Bing's Grocery in town. As soon as she mentioned fruitcakes from Sweet Delights Bakery, he interrupted her.

"That's a fantastic recipe!" he exclaimed. "I just had a slice at my niece's house the other day. I'd love to carry those in my store. What were you thinking for my cost?"

Lucy hesitated, then suggested the figure she'd come up with. For a moment, Danny was silent, and Lucy chewed her lip, wondering if she'd gone too high.

"Just punching that into my calculator," he murmured, and Lucy held her breath.

A moment later, he made a "hmm…" sound and she clutched the phone nervously. She was totally unprepared for what he said next.

"Sounds good! Can you supply fifty cakes by Thursday?"

Lucy gulped. That was the day after tomorrow.

She closed her eyes briefly, wondering if Hannah was going to kill her.

"Sure," she confirmed, in a voice full of cheer. "No problem at all."

4

Lucy and Hannah worked well into the evening, and both arrived at dawn the next morning to continue baking. After a quick run into town to replenish their stock of candied fruit, production continued, and finished fruitcakes soon covered every available inch of space in the bakery's kitchen.

Aunt Tricia and Betsy took care of packaging the cooled cakes, in between waiting on customers, carefully placing the pink and black Sweet Delights labels on top of the cellophane. With everyone pitching in, the crew had the entire order complete by late Thursday morning.

"Whew!" Hannah sank into a chair out front. "I wouldn't mind not seeing another fruitcake until next Christmas."

Lucy smirked. "Better close your eyes, then, because you need to help me deliver them to Bing's later."

Hannah chuckled. "Seeing that I have no space to work in the kitchen until they're gone, I'm agreeable to that."

Betsy marveled, shaking her head. "You guys just knocked those out, like you were a fruitcake factory. Suddenly, my plan to bake a triple batch of Christmas cookies at home this weekend seems less daunting."

"Your mom and dad would be proud," Aunt Tricia said, smiling at Lucy and Hannah. The two exchanged pleased looks at the compliment.

"Speaking of Christmas plans," Lucy said, "I asked Taylor when he was free to go to Nelson Farm, and he said tomorrow evening. Is everyone good with that?"

"Sounds great!" said Hannah, standing up and stretching and yawning.

"Oh, goody!" Betsy clasped her hands, looking excited. "Joseph and I were already getting together tomorrow night, so I know he's free. This will be so much fun!"

Hannah walked wearily back toward the kitchen, saying, "I still need to make a batch of buttercream icing. Let me know when you want to go to Bing's, Lucy."

Lucy stood as well, intending to go up to her office to do some paperwork, but suddenly she saw Taylor's police car pulling into the parking lot.

"Look who's here," Aunt Tricia said with a smile, noticing the same thing. "I bet that boy needs an apple turnover."

She walked behind the pastry case, readying a takeout bag. Taylor had a sweet tooth and was particularly enamored of apple turnovers.

The bell jangled as the deputy came in. His handsome face broke into a devilish grin, and he called out loudly, "I need twenty fruitcakes by four o'clock!"

He laughed heartily as Hannah instantly popped her head back through the archway with a look of dismay.

"Oh, very funny," she said, upon seeing Taylor. She made a silly face at him before disappearing into the kitchen again.

Lucy chuckled and crossed to him for a quick hug, drawing back to look up into his face. "I was just telling the girls we're good to go to Nelson Farm tomorrow night."

Taylor nodded, his blue eyes capturing hers. "All finished with the massive fruitcake order?" he asked softly, and Lucy nodded.

"Good job," he said, giving her shoulder a squeeze. He said hello to Betsy and approached the counter to greet Aunt Tricia, while Lucy busied herself erasing the morning specials from the chalkboard.

"How's your morning going, Taylor?" asked Aunt Tricia, pouring him a coffee to go.

Taylor sighed, tucking his thumbs into his front pockets. "Not as well as it could be. I found myself chasing down Al Forrester first thing this morning to give him one last warning."

Lucy glanced over, frowning. "Isn't that Heather Kelly's ex-husband?"

Taylor nodded, his expression hardening.

Aunt Tricia asked, "Warn him? About what?" She handed Taylor the bag with his pastry.

Taylor murmured his thanks and answered, "The man won't leave Heather alone. Ever since she got engaged to Jonas Nelson, he's been following her, sitting in his car outside her house, calling her to beg for another chance."

Lucy looked surprised. "But they've been divorced for years, haven't they?"

Aunt Tricia nodded in confirmation. "Five years, if I remember correctly. Seems to me he'd realize that ship has already sailed."

Lucy asked Taylor, worry in her voice. "Is this guy violent? Is Heather in danger?"

Taylor shook his head. "He's never been violent, but you never know. Sometimes people just snap. I told him this is his last warning. Heather's ready to file a restraining order against him."

"Oh, my," said Aunt Tricia, clucking her tongue. "Well, perhaps he'll leave her be, now that you've spoken to him."

"I sure hope so," Taylor replied, picking up his coffee cup. "Well, I've got to get back to work. So, tomorrow night at seven?" He looked at Lucy for confirmation.

She nodded with a smile. "Yes. Betsy and Joseph and Hannah will be coming, too."

Taylor grinned. "The more the merrier!" He headed out the door, calling out his goodbyes.

Just as he left, another customer came in.

It was Mrs. White, one of Sweet Delights' best customers. She came in at least twice a week to pick up pastries for her family, and ordered all her birthday cakes with Lucy, too. She was also a notorious gossip, though a good-hearted woman.

"Mrs. White," Lucy greeted her. "What can we get for you today?"

The woman unwound the sparkling pastel-colored scarf from her neck, draping it over her arm. "Goodness, it's cold out there! You know, ladies, it's supposed to snow this weekend!" She pulled out her phone from an oversized purse.

"I've made a list of what I need for holiday pies. It's on here somewhere…" She punched a few buttons on the phone and looked confused, scrolling through apps.

Betsy scooted behind the counter, a pen and order pad at the ready. Suddenly, Mrs. White's phone chimed with a Christmas ringtone, "Let it Snow".

The woman looked up at Betsy and Lucy apologetically. "Oh, that's my sister! Excuse me for one moment." She stepped away from the counter and spoke briefly into the phone.

Betsy and Lucy exchanged worried glances as Mrs. White cried out, "Oh, no! That's terrible!"

Aunt Tricia cocked her head and whispered to Lucy, "What's terrible?"

Lucy shook her head, at a loss.

Mrs. White said a few more words and hung up, returning to the counter. She fussed with her phone, tucking it away and then pulling it back out, obviously flustered.

She glanced at their expectant faces and shook her head regretfully. "That was my sister, Dora. You know, she's the music teacher at Ivy Creek Elementary…"

Lucy, Betsy, and Aunt Tricia all nodded, waiting to hear what had happened.

Mrs. White's face was fraught with dismay as she shared her bad news.

"Dora's got the flu. They're going to have to cancel the Christmas Choral Concert!"

5

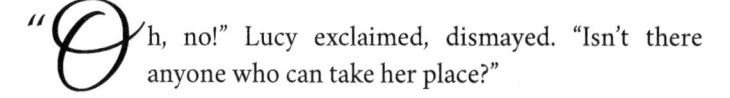

"Oh, no!" Lucy exclaimed, dismayed. "Isn't there anyone who can take her place?"

Aunt Tricia asked, referring to a third-grade teacher, "How about Mrs. Gallow? She has some musical background."

Mrs. White shook her head, "Mrs. Gallow is in Montana, visiting her grandchildren until after New Year's." She clucked her tongue, looked down at her phone in her hand, and once again returned it to her purse.

"I'll have to call in that pie order, dear," she told Lucy, her face lined with worry. "I can't even think straight. I need to make a big pot of chicken soup for Dora. Yes, that's what I'll do. Oh, the poor thing..." Mrs. White wandered away, still shaking her head over the news.

The bell jangled as she left, and Lucy looked at Betsy and Aunt Tricia.

"That would be such a shame," Lucy said. "Half the town is looking forward to that concert."

Aunt Tricia sighed. "Oh, the poor children! They'll be so disappointed."

Betsy bit her lip, and ventured, "I have an idea…"

The other ladies turned to face her.

Betsy continued, "I'll have to ask Joseph, but you know, the theater doesn't have another show until after the new year. And Joseph studied music in college. It's possible he could step in as musical director for the concert."

Lucy smiled at her. "That would be wonderful! Go call him now, Betsy, if you don't mind, before they call the whole thing off."

Betsy grinned. "Fingers crossed!" She picked up the phone and walked to the other side of the bakery.

"Oh, my," Aunt Tricia murmured. "I do hope that Joseph can take that on." She turned to neaten the stack of packaged fudge on the counter, displaced from its usual table.

"Are you delivering the fruitcakes to Bing's soon?" she asked Lucy, surveying the bakery's interior, the tabletops crowded with the festively packaged products. "The customers won't have much seating if we get a lunch rush, with the veranda closed for the winter."

Lucy nodded, looking at the clock. "I've just got to get the invoice ready and check in with Hannah."

Twenty minutes later, Lucy and Hannah were finishing up loading the bakery's van, shivering despite their jackets.

Hannah looked up at the sky with a frown. "Gee, I'd hate for our excursion to Nelson Farm tomorrow night to get snowed out."

Lucy chuckled as they hopped inside and buckled their seatbelts. "Such a snow-hater," she teased her friend. "Don't worry, both Taylor and Joseph have four-wheel drive."

They started down the street, with Hannah admiring the Christmas decorations in the neighboring yards. She turned to Lucy with a sudden thought.

"Who should I ride with? You and Taylor, or Betsy and Joseph?"

Lucy shrugged, her eyes on the road. "Either one. Whichever you prefer. We all live pretty close."

Hannah pondered her response and sighed. "Either way, I'll feel like a fifth wheel." She sighed, and Lucy glanced at her friend with sympathy.

"Any new prospects on the dating front?" she asked. She knew Hannah had been on several dates over the summer, but none of the men seemed to suit her.

Hannah shook her head. "No one exciting," she replied. "I guess it'll be just me and Spooky on New Year's Eve."

Lucy immediately offered, "You can always join me and Taylor, if you want." She didn't like the thought of Hannah sitting at home alone on New Year's Eve. Although Lucy knew Hannah always spent Christmas with her mom and dad, she hadn't thought much about New Year's, yet.

Hannah chuckled. "On New Year's Eve? Then I'd really feel like a fifth wheel!" She smiled at Lucy. "Thanks, but I'll be fine."

They turned onto the street for Bing's Grocery, and Lucy instructed, "Help me look for a spot out front, please. It's too far to park in the back lot."

She slowed down, glad there was no one right on her tail, and searched for a space.

"There's one!" Hannah pointed. It was really in front of the tavern next door, but Lucy thought it was the best they would find. She edged into the spot, having to make two tries of back and forth to get it right, but then finally was satisfied.

The girls got out and Lucy said, "We'll grab a couple carts once we're in there, but there's no sense going in with empty hands."

She opened the sliding door of the van and loaded Hannah's arms up first, then grabbed the invoice and a stack of fruitcakes for herself.

Hannah chuckled as the two walked towards the store, carefully balancing twin towers of packaged cakes. "If Bing's orders another round, maybe we should have them pick them up!"

Lucy grinned. "Oh? Does that mean you're up for baking another fifty cakes next week?"

Hannah groaned. "Forget I said anything."

As they passed the tavern's door, Lucy noticed a man lounging in front on the sidewalk. He looked at them with slitted eyes as they passed, and she felt an overwhelming air of malice in his gaze. She glanced away quickly, sliding a look at Hannah, but her friend was looking down, trying to avoid bumps on the sidewalk.

Lucy was grateful for the automatic sliding door as they entered Bing's Grocery. Within minutes, they had located the manager, who accepted the invoice and pointed them in the direction of an empty table near the deli.

The ladies unloaded themselves of the packaged cakes and grabbed two shopping carts as they left the store. They pushed the noisy carts down the sidewalk, and Lucy saw the ominous character was still standing in front of the tavern.

A moment after they'd passed him, Hannah whispered to Lucy, "Did you see that guy?"

Lucy nodded as they reached the van. "He's definitely not from around here. He looks dangerous."

She opened the van's side door, and the two began loading their carts.

"He looked like mob to me," Hannah mused.

Lucy frowned. "Mob? In Ivy Creek?" She was skeptical.

Hannah clarified, "Well, not from here, but there's organized crime running rampant through Lowell, you know. And we're not far from there."

Lucy pondered this as they finished loading the carts. She stacked cakes upon cakes, grateful for the density of the fruitcake, protecting them from crushing.

"I wonder why he's in Ivy Creek, just hanging around?" Lucy slid the door shut and locked the van. The ladies steered their carts towards Bing's again, the wheels clattering on the bumpy sidewalk.

Her rhetorical question was answered a moment later, as they drew abreast of the tavern's entrance once again. A patron was emerging from the dimly lit establishment, and the stranger stepped in front of the man, blocking his path.

He scowled and jabbed a finger at the other man's chest. His gravelly voice could be heard as Lucy and Hannah rattled past with their carts full of cakes, his tone dire with warning.

"Hey, pal. You see your buddy Jonas, you better tell him Vic is looking for him."

6

Lucy and Hannah exchanged worried glances but kept moving. By tacit agreement, they didn't speak until a minute later, after they'd passed through the doors of Bing's Grocery.

Hannah cast a nervous glance behind them, then looked at Lucy with her eyes wide. "Did you hear that? Do you think it was Jonas Nelson that guy was looking for?"

Lucy compressed her lips, concerned at the implications. "I really hope not." She knew Jonas had run with the wrong crowd in his younger days, but it had been many years since he'd been in any trouble.

"Hmm. Well, I don't know any other Jonas in Ivy Creek," Hannah pointed out, as they reached their table and began to arrange the cakes in a pyramid.

Lucy knew her friend was right. She wondered if she should mention the dangerous-looking man to Taylor. She hated to bother him, especially since it wasn't really her place to step into Jonas Nelson's business. And the stranger hadn't committed a crime. She just got a bad vibe from him.

The ladies finished their display, and Lucy stepped back to admire their work. Seeing Sweet Delights Bakery's pink and black logos peeking out, all through the small tower of cakes, she was filled with a rush of pride. She hoped her mother would have approved of selling at Bing's. All in all, Lucy felt like she'd made a lot of progress for the bakery in the last couple of years.

Putting all thoughts of the ominous stranger out of her head for the moment, Lucy grinned at Hannah, saying, "Well done, my friend!"

They turned from the display, and after a brief stop at the office, the women exited the store, both zipping up their jackets against the chilly breeze.

When they passed by the tavern, the stranger was gone, and neither Lucy nor Hannah mentioned him on the way home.

"Here they are!" Hannah announced, peeking out through the curtain of Lucy and Aunt Tricia's living room.

Joseph's dark blue SUV pulled in behind Taylor's vehicle, and Betsy waved, leaning out the window as Lucy, Hannah, and Taylor approached.

"Isn't it a beautiful night?" Betsy marveled, her cheeks blooming with pink. "I told Joseph I thought I saw snowflakes on the way over!"

Aunt Tricia could be heard calling from the porch steps. "You guys be careful, now, if it begins to snow. Those roads can get icy, quick!"

Taylor turned his head to smile at her. "Yes, ma'am"

Joseph rolled down his window. "Hi, Tricia. You bet we will! But Betsy imagined the snowflakes…" He laughed as Betsy mock-punched his arm.

"I did not!" Her eyes sparkled with humor.

Taylor opened his vehicle's doors for Hannah and Lucy, and soon the trio was backing out of the driveway, waving goodbye to Aunt Tricia. Lucy leaned back, sighing, happy to watch the lit-up houses as they passed by.

"Oh, look at that one!" Hannah pointed to an elaborate display on a neighboring front lawn.

Lucy smiled at the house with a wonderland scene in their yard. Twinkling lights were wound around conical evergreen trees, and reindeer statues appeared to be nibbling at the grass through the patchy snow. Giant candy cane posts marched along either side of the driveway, and an inflatable Santa wobbled near the front door, rocking gently in the light breeze.

Lucy glanced at Taylor. "Do you remember caroling in high school?" She and Taylor, and a few of their other friends had made a tradition of caroling in Lucy's neighborhood. Hannah's family lived on the other side of town, so she'd not participated.

Taylor grinned at her, his blue eyes sparkling. "I sure do! I remember you made me that scarf. I still wear it, you know."

Lucy smiled fondly at him, thinking of their history together. He'd been her first real boyfriend in high school, and she'd undertaken the knitting of a scarf for him with great enthusiasm, although she'd been new to the craft. She recalled staying up long past midnight on many a night, determined to have it ready before the first snow. She'd presented it to him as an early Christmas gift, and he'd kissed her so sweetly, standing beneath the mistletoe.

Taylor's eyes crinkled and he teased her, glancing between her face and the road. "I know what you're remembering…"

Lucy blushed and laughed, caught.

Hannah remarked dryly, "Not to intrude on a private moment, but look, guys! It's starting to snow! Betsy was right!"

Lucy turned to look back through the windshield, spotting the frozen flakes spiraling down, floating past the glass. They looked magical in the wash of the car's headlights.

"How perfect!" Lucy announced and reached for Taylor's hand, giving it a squeeze. He winked at her.

A moment later, Joseph was pulling into the parking lot of Nelson Farm. Rows of Fraser fir trees were arranged in a huge quadrant just behind the Nelson Farm Stand, a cozy wooden building decorated with festive colored lights. Jonas's modest mobile home was located at the end of a dirt driveway on one side of the field, and the Nelson's sprawling family farmhouse and barn were on the other side.

The parking lot had a smattering of cars, and Lucy could see Lenora Nelson through the windows of the farm stand, talking to customers.

Lucy turned to her friends. "Let's pop in and say hello to Mrs. Nelson before we start tree-hunting," she suggested.

Taylor and Hannah agreed, and they climbed out of the vehicle. Betsy and Joseph were waiting next to his SUV. Betsy was standing with her face upturned to the sky, wearing a huge grin as she watched the fat flakes drifting down.

"I told you guys!" she crowed, and the others chuckled. They began moving toward the entrance.

"Sure smells good in here!" Taylor remarked, holding the door open for the group.

Lucy stopped just inside the entrance, closing her eyes, and letting the Christmasy scent wash over her–a combination of evergreen, gingerbread and cinnamon. She smiled as she opened them again. If only she could bottle the scent of Christmas!

She saw Mrs. Nelson was still chatting with a customer, so she wandered through the store, admiring the displays. Hannah and Betsy were going through the selection of wreaths, and Taylor and Joseph stood together off to one side, debating the best method of securing Christmas trees to the vehicles' roofs: rope or tie-down straps.

Lucy saw the display of dog cookies and walked over to the small table, her interest piqued.

She picked one up, approving of its heft, and set it back down. *If only Mrs. Nelson was making cat treats! Gigi sure loved her "kitty candies".*

"Hi there, Lucy!" Lenora Nelson approached her with a smile. "I see you've found my dog cookies. What do you think?"

"They look great!" Lucy said with a grin, then teased, "How does Ivan feel about you baking cookies for all the other dogs?"

She'd met Ivan a time or two before, but he was usually glued to Jonas's side. He was a large black dog, some sort of shepherd-lab mix that the Nelsons had rescued as a stray.

Mrs. Nelson's smile dimmed somewhat at the mention of the canine. "I'm not sure where Ivan is," she admitted. "I've been calling him since his dinner time, but he hasn't come scratching on the door yet."

She glanced out the window with concern. "And now it's starting to snow. To tell you the truth, I'm beginning to get a little worried."

7

"Worried about who?" Taylor appeared at Lucy's side. "Hi, Mrs. Nelson."

Lenora greeted him, as well as the rest of the gang, as they wandered over. "Oh, I'm sure it's nothing. I was just telling Lucy our farm dog is late for dinner."

"We'll keep an eye out for him," Taylor assured her. "Doesn't he usually hang out with Jonas? We're headed out to the Christmas trees next."

Lenora smiled. "What a wonderful evening to buy a tree!" She looked out the window where the snowflakes had started to come down heavier. "I better let you guys get to it, before the roads get slippery." She turned away, adding over her shoulder. "When you see Jonas, please remind him if he sees Ivan, to shut him into the barn tonight, because of the weather."

"Will do," Lucy promised. She looked at her friends. "Ready to go tree hunting?"

"Absolutely!" Betsy beamed. Joseph nodded, reaching over to zip up Betsy's coat.

Hannah put her hat back on. "I'm not getting a tree, but I'll help you guys find yours."

Together, the group exited the store, standing for a moment in the swirling snow. A family with two small children walked past, with the father lugging their new tree over to his truck.

Lucy smiled at the delight on the children's faces, overhearing one of them ask their mother if they could stay up late and decorate the tree tonight.

"I just love Christmas!" Betsy announced, turning her face up to the sky. "And a white Christmas would be even more perfect!"

They began to walk to the Christmas tree section, lit up with more twinkling lights.

Hannah turned up her collar. "The snow falling does make for a pretty picture," she agreed with a shiver. "But why does it have to be so cold?"

Taylor glanced down at Lucy as they walked together. "Are you warm enough?" he asked in a low tone. His voice was full of tenderness, and a blush rose to her cheeks.

She nodded and squeezed his hand in her mittened one. "Yes, thank you, I'm toasty."

They stopped at a large table, set up beneath a banner advertising the tree prices. A sizeable airpot was set up next to a stack of Styrofoam cups, with a sign offering "Free Hot Chocolate".

Lucy looked around, mildly surprised when she didn't spot Jonas or Ivan. Jonas always worked the Christmas tree stand.

"Do you want hot chocolate?" Joseph asked Betsy. She shook her head.

"I want to go find our tree first. Maybe afterward."

"Well, I do. I need a warm-up." Hannah stepped forward, selecting a cup and dispensing some of the hot beverage.

The fragrant steam rising through the air made Lucy's mouth water, but she decided, she too, would wait until after they found their tree. The snow was coming down harder, and it was beginning to stick. She didn't want Aunt Tricia to worry about them.

"Stick together, or split up?" Joseph asked, scanning the huge quadrant of trees, set up in rows.

Taylor grinned. "Let's go in different directions and see who finds the best-looking tree."

Lucy regarded him with amusement. *Of course, the men would make this into a competition.*

"You're on!" Joseph said with a gleam in his eye. He and Betsy veered to the left, soon disappearing from sight among the snow-covered evergreens.

"I'm going to look for Ivan," Hannah announced. "But if I see an absolutely perfect tree, I'll call out."

"OK." Lucy smiled at Taylor, and they began their hunt.

They moved slowly through the rows of trees. The Fraser firs stood so tall and full, Lucy had the illusion she was truly in a forest. The evergreens' scent made her nostalgic, conjuring visions of visiting Nelson Farm with her father every year, searching for a perfect tree to take home to Mother.

"How about this one?" Taylor stopped next to a burly specimen, admiring its fullness.

Lucy eyed it, trying to picture it in her living room. "Nice, but I think it's too short," she decreed, and continued strolling along.

A short distance away, she found one she liked. "Hey, what about this one?"

Taylor joined her and nodded. "Very nice." He swiveled the tree around to see the backside, and Lucy was disappointed to see a bare patch.

"Oh… maybe not," she said.

Taylor spun the tree again, regarding the perfect front side. "Well, no one will see the back, remember, up against the wall."

Lucy considered the tree, head tilted, and acknowledged his words with a nod. "Let's keep it in mind. We can always backtrack."

They continued on toward the end of the first row, finding several that were contenders, but Lucy always found some small flaw. The branches started too low on this one; they ended too abruptly at the top on that one. This one lacked a pyramid shape, another one was not vividly green enough.

Taylor chuckled as they came to the end of the second row. "If we keep this up, we're going to run into Joseph and Betsy on the other side," he joked.

Lucy grinned and pointed out, "Well, Joseph hasn't called out yet that they've found one, either. Betsy must be as picky as I am."

Taylor raised his eyebrows. "So, it would seem."

Lucy tucked her arm in his as they rounded the corner. "OK, if we don't find the perfect tree in this row, we can go back and grab that other one." She peeked up at Taylor's face, hoping he wasn't getting impatient.

His blue eyes crinkled as he smiled down at her. "I'm not in a rush," he said. "In fact, it's kind of nice, wandering through a winter wonderland with you."

Lucy felt a rush of affection at his words and squeezed his arm in response. She was enjoying herself as well. Suddenly, she felt Taylor stiffen, and abruptly come to a stop.

She looked up, confused. "What is it?" She glanced at his face, and turned, following his gaze.

Bracketed by rows of Fraser firs, a figure lay still and silent across the path, dark against the growing blanket of white. Snowflakes drifted gently down, settling on the man's hair and clothing.

Lucy zeroed in on the dark blue parka, filled with horror as she realized who it was.

"That's Jonas!"

8

*L*ucy and Taylor rushed forward at once, crouching in the snow beside the man. Taylor called Jonas by name, patting his cheeks, and reaching for the man's arm to check his pulse.

Lucy pulled out her phone with shaking hands, dialing 911. The snow was settling on Jonas's frozen face, and Lucy knew the truth, even before Taylor spoke. There was no pulse.

Taylor started CPR, and Lucy turned away, tears freezing on her cheeks as she spoke to the 911 operator.

Betsy, Hannah, and Joseph came around the corner just as Lucy hung up the phone.

"Oh my God, who is that?" Hannah ran forward, alarmed. Taylor stopped his ministrations, knowing it was no use.

"It's Jonas," Lucy answered, her voice dulled by sadness, watching Taylor gently shut Jonas's eyes.

"The ambulance is on the way," she added lamely. It didn't matter now.

Hannah sank down on her knees in the snow, shocked, and Betsy hid her face in Joseph's coat, trembling.

Taylor looked at Lucy's face, noting her pallor. "Joseph, please take the girls out to the parking lot," he requested, his face grim. "I'll wait here until the paramedics come."

Joseph ushered them away, and Lucy glanced back once over her shoulder, unable to comprehend that Jonas Nelson was really dead.

They reached the parking area and Lucy saw the lot was now empty except for Taylor and Joseph's vehicles. The Christmas tree station was still lit up, but the farm stand had been closed up for the night, the cheery yellow glow missing from its windows, now shuttered against the storm.

Lenora must have gone back to the farmhouse, Lucy realized, a little ashamed by the relief she felt for not having to break the news to the woman, herself.

Within minutes, several cruisers and an ambulance had arrived, their flashing lights coloring the falling snowflakes blue and red. The lights came on at the farmhouse and Lucy knew Lenora must have seen the commotion. An officer was dispatched to the house to inform her of the terrible news, while the gang waited for Taylor, speaking in hushed tones, overwhelmed with shock.

Over at Jonas's trailer, there was activity as well. Lucy watched as the headlights of a vehicle came on, and it traveled down the long driveway toward them.

There was a flurry of activity as the paramedics appeared, carrying Jonas's lifeless body out of the field on a stretcher, his face covered with a sheet.

Taylor joined them, his face tight with suppressed emotion. Lucy knew this death was hitting him hard, the same as it was her. This wasn't a stranger. Jonas Nelson had been someone they all knew very well.

Lucy wrapped her arms around Taylor's waist in a tight embrace, and he hugged her back. Stepping away to look into his face, she asked, "How did it happen? Can you tell?"

Taylor shook his head. "The coroner will have to tell us. There wasn't a mark on him."

Suddenly, several vehicles pulled into the parking lot, one right after the other. Lucy watched helplessly as Lenora Nelson emerged from one, a long coat thrown hastily over her dressing gown. She ran to the stretcher with a cry of anguish, her hands outstretched.

"My baby! No, no, I have to see him," she begged, as a paramedic tried to catch hold of her arms.

Taylor nodded to the man, and Lenora stood by, clutching her collar, as Taylor carefully peeled the sheet back from Jonas's face.

Lenora sobbed as she looked at her son. "My poor boy." She turned to Taylor. "But how? How did it happen?" Bewilderment was evident on her face and in her voice.

Taylor gently took hold of Lenora's hands, the compassion in his face breaking Lucy's heart. "We don't know yet, Mrs. Nelson," he told her gently. "But we'll find out."

Her voice trembled. "Was he killed? Was it an accident? Or… something else?"

Taylor shook his head, repeating softly, "We really don't know anything yet. But we're not ruling anything out."

Lucy approached Mrs. Nelson, laying a hand on the woman's arm. "Is there someone we can call for you? You shouldn't be alone right now. One of the kids?"

Most of the Nelson brood lived spread out over the property, everyone helping out with the farm when they could, though all but Jonas had taken jobs in the city. Lucy was surprised none of them had seen the lights yet and come to investigate.

Mrs. Nelson retrieved a handkerchief from her pocket and wiped at her eyes as Jonas's body was carried away on the stretcher. She shook her head. "Dominic will be here soon. Kira and Jason are out of town for the weekend."

Lucy nodded, watching the ambulance leave. She wondered briefly if she should call Aunt Tricia. As soon as she'd had that thought, she dismissed it, not wanting her aunt out driving in the storm.

A stranger approached and Lucy eyed the man, trying to place him, but was unable to. He appeared to be in his late fifties and was dressed in a leather duster and gray wool hat and mittens.

"What's happened?" the man demanded of Taylor, without acknowledging Lenora. "Why are the police here?"

Lenora whirled around at the sound of the man's voice, her face filled with fury.

"You! You did this, didn't you?" She accused him, her shrill voice carrying on the wind. "I remember you threatened my boy! You said he'd regret it if he went ahead with the lawsuit!"

She turned to Taylor, in a state of near hysteria. "Arrest him! I don't know how he managed it, but mark my words, if there was foul play involved, then Chad Prentiss is responsible! I know it...." Her voice cracked on the last word, and Lucy put her arm around the woman's shoulders, patting her back, trying to comfort her.

The man scowled, stepping away from Mrs. Nelson. He faced Taylor, his expression one of disdain. "She's off her rocker," he insisted. "I haven't done anything to anyone."

Taylor's demeanor remained professional as he acknowledged the man's words with a quiet suggestion. "Mr... Prentiss, is it? Why don't you go on home now, and if the police have any questions, we'll come by and talk to you."

The man frowned. "I don't know why you'd have any questions for me," he countered, stubbornly, folding his arms. "What happened here? Did something happen to Jonas?"

Taylor raised his eyebrows, nodding in the direction of the man's car. "Please, sir."

The man turned on his heel and stomped away, getting into his car and leaving. Lucy looked over Mrs. Nelson's head at Taylor, her eyes wide. She felt Hannah come up behind her and wondered if her friend had heard the exchange.

Hannah spoke gently, "Mrs. Nelson, Dominic just arrived. He's over there talking to a policeman. May I escort you to him?"

Mrs. Nelson nodded gratefully, dabbing at her eyes, and Lucy gave her friend a look of thanks, as she led the grieving mother away.

Taylor sighed, looking after them, then his concerned gaze connected with Lucy's. "I'm going to be a while, I'm afraid. I think Joseph should take you and Hannah home."

Lucy nodded, shivering as the wind picked up. "Please be careful driving home, Taylor. The roads are probably going to get worse."

He nodded, dropping a brief kiss on her forehead. "I will."

Lucy began to turn away but stopped as a young woman in a white coat and red hat hurried over to her. Her face was tear-stained, her nose red. Lucy recognized the woman by her long, ash blonde hair.

"Oh, Heather," Lucy hugged Jonas's fiancé tightly, realizing now it was Heather who'd been leaving Jonas's house. "I'm so sorry!"

Heather looked at Taylor, her expression shellshocked. "Is it true? Is Jonas... dead?"

Taylor nodded his head. "I'm sorry," he said simply.

Heather's eyes streamed tears, and she shuddered and wiped them away. "I can't believe it," she said, her voice raw with emotion.

She turned to face Taylor again, a grim expression settling over her delicate features.

"Was he murdered?" Before Taylor could reply, she hurried on. "I heard Lenora accusing Chad Prentiss of threatening Jonas."

She looked between Lucy and Taylor, her next words shocking them both.

"If Jonas *was* murdered, I think my ex-husband may be responsible."

9

Taylor frowned. "Al? Do you have cause to believe Al would harm Jonas?"

Heather looked troubled. "You know he's been harassing me, but I never told you, he's been harassing Jonas as well."

Taylor compressed his lips. "In what way?"

The woman's light blue eyes filled up with fresh tears. "He's been leaving notes on Jonas's car, when he's stayed over at my house. Jonas thought he'd been followed by Al a few times, too."

Taylor sighed. "Heather, you should have told me this the last time we talked. I would have brought it up to Al when I warned him to stay away from you."

Lucy asked, brow furrowed. "What did the notes say, Heather?"

Heather wiped at her tears with a mittened hand. "Um… some stuff about not getting between a man and his wife, that sort of thing." She looked at Taylor, her eyes filled with despair. "I know I should have told you, but Jonas said he'd handle it himself." Her breath caught on a sob, and Lucy rubbed her arm consolingly.

Taylor looked over to where Dominic and Lenora stood together, talking to another officer.

"Heather, I'd feel better if you didn't drive right now. Any chance you could stay over at Lenora's house?"

Heather sniffled and nodded. "I'm sure she wouldn't mind."

Taylor nodded at Lucy. "I'll stop by the bakery tomorrow," he told her, softly, before tucking Heather's hand in the crook of his arm and leading her across the icy parking lot.

Joseph and Betsy were huddled nearby, and Lucy joined them, signaling to Hannah across the lot. Within minutes, they were all bundled into Joseph's SUV, with his tires crunching on icy snow as they exited the parking lot.

Lucy cast a look behind them through the back windshield, watching the twinkling lights of Nelson Farm fade into the distance. She wondered if tonight's tragedy would forever taint her joy of coming here to pick out a Christmas tree.

"I JUST CAN'T BELIEVE IT," Aunt Tricia's eyes were red, but she'd managed to stop the flow of tears. She sighed with a heavy heart, gazing unseeing out the bakery's window, at the fresh blanket of snow.

Betsy, however, had to keep excusing herself as a fresh wave of sorrow would overtake her. She could be heard crying in the restroom. Though she didn't know Jonas well, she'd explained to Lucy that the experience last night, so close to Christmas, had triggered something in her.

Lucy understood completely. The shock of losing a loved one was something everyone could relate to, and at this time of year, it seemed an especially cruel twist of fate.

Taylor had stopped by first thing this morning, and the news he'd shared had only made the situation more unsettling. Although they were waiting upon the coroner's final report, he said they'd already ruled out natural causes, such as a heart attack, stroke, or aneurysm. Lucy could tell from Taylor's tone of voice that he was troubled at the prospect of another murder in Ivy Creek.

"Have they questioned Al Forrester?" Hannah asked, coming into the front space from the kitchen. She began arranging freshly baked pastries in the case.

Lucy shook her head. "I didn't get a chance to ask Taylor. I imagine they will, though, based on what Heather said last night."

"How could anyone take that young man's life and just leave him there in the snow?" Aunt Tricia's voice quavered. "I just don't understand what's happened to this world."

Lucy tried to soothe her. "Now, Auntie, we don't know for sure what happened. Try not to dwell too much on it. It's bad for your heart."

Aunt Tricia gave a decidedly un-ladylike snort. "What's worse for my poor heart is to see this town gone crazy. I tell you, I'd never have believed in my wildest dreams that Ivy Creek would have become such a hotbed of murders. This sleepy little town..." she shook her head sadly. "I remember the good old days. Why, I don't think your uncle

Harry and I ever locked our doors, back when you were a child."

"Ivy Creek's not that bad," Betsy said in a small voice, having just emerged from the ladies' room. "I think, on the whole, most of the people who live here are good souls." She turned to look at Lucy hopefully. "Don't you think so?"

Lucy hesitated just briefly, and then nodded, if only to dispel the black mood hanging over them. It was true there had been a rash of murders in Ivy Creek in the last two years. Some of the murders had even been committed by longtime residents, as was the case of Clara Davidson, the town's librarian, who'd killed a famous author in a jealous rage, and had almost gotten away with it.

Aunt Tricia rose from her chair, sighing. "Well, things are different now. That's all I know. I sure do miss those simpler times." She picked up her cup and walked back behind the counter, busying herself with organizing the rolls of register tape.

Lucy looked after her, troubled by her aunt's melancholy. It seemed more and more lately that Aunt Tricia was spending her time reminiscing about the old days, rather than getting out to have new experiences. Although, it was true, Lucy reflected, that her aunt had recently formed a book club. But even her book club meetings seemed to spark discussions of how the past was preferable to the present.

Lucy drummed her fingers on the table, looking out the window at the snow, unable to focus on her work today. What could she do to bring Aunt Tricia out of her sad mood?

She suddenly remembered the idea she'd had the other night for Aunt Tricia's Christmas present. If only she could find one of those antique ceramic trees somewhere! As nostalgic as Aunt Tricia was feeling lately, it would be the perfect Christmas gift.

Lucy stood and pushed her chair back in, filled with new resolve. She had the internet at her fingertips, with eBay, and Etsy, and a whole host of other online markets.

Surely, if she put her mind to it, she'd be able to find an Atlantic ceramic tree before the holiday was upon them.

10

"I called earlier and spoke to Dominic," Aunt Tricia said, as they drove up the driveway to the Nelson farmhouse. "He said to stop by anytime."

Lucy nodded, glad that Mrs. Nelson had family around her to offer their support. She and Aunt Tricia had baked two casseroles to bring to the family in their time of grieving.

As they exited Lucy's car, the front door of the farmhouse opened, and a young woman peered out. Lucy waved, recognizing Lenora's daughter, Kira. As they approached the house, Kira was joined by her brother Dominic.

"Thank you for thinking of us," he said, as he and Kira accepted the casseroles. His face was drawn and pale, but he seemed to be holding up as well as could be expected.

Kira led them down the hallway to the sitting room. "Mother's in here," she said, gesturing through the door.

Lenora rose from her chair as Lucy and Aunt Tricia entered the room. She was dressed all in black. Her face was composed, though a mask of grief had settled over her features, adding ten years to her appearance. She held out her hands as Aunt Tricia came forward, and the two embraced.

"Lenora, I am so, so, sorry, for your loss," Aunt Tricia said sadly, looking into her friend's dark-eyed gaze. "There are no words to express how much I wish your family had been spared this."

Lenora smiled sadly, and Lucy gave her a quick hug, echoing Aunt Tricia's sentiment.

"If there's anything we can do, Mrs. Nelson, please don't hesitate to ask."

Lenora nodded, her lips trembling, but she quickly composed herself, indicating that they should sit.

"Thank you for taking the time to visit," she said, settling back down in the wing-back chair. "Honestly, I'm still in shock. I keep thinking this is a bad dream, and I'll wake up and Jonas will be here." She dabbed at her eyes quickly, keeping her tears at bay.

Aunt Tricia leaned forward and asked, gently, "Have you heard anything from the police yet?"

Lenora shook her head. "Dominic is in touch with them several times a day, but apparently, the cause of death has not yet been determined." Her face darkened. "It's looking more and more like murder, though, as they've ruled out most natural causes of death."

Lucy bit her lip, tempted to ask more about Mrs. Nelson's accusing words the night Jonas was found, aimed at Chad Prentiss, but decided to stay quiet.

Aunt Tricia patted her friend's knee. "I'm glad Dominic is here to deal with the police, and that Kira's with you as well. Let your children be a comfort to you, Lenora. You need to focus on resting." She studied Lenora's haunted eyes. "Are you sleeping at all?"

Lenora offered a wry smile. "Not as much as I'd like to. To be honest, I'm feeling so shaky from lack of sleep. I may have to go see Doc Timmons for a sedative prescription."

She looked out the parlor window, her thoughts drifting. "I received a call this morning from an auction house, specializing in estate sales, but it hurts too much to think about that, just yet."

Lucy spoke up. "Maybe Dominic or Kira could handle that for you."

Lenora nodded her head. "Yes, but my brain is so muddled, I forgot to ask the caller for contact information. I just told him, now was not a good time. Maybe he'll call back."

Aunt Tricia frowned slightly. "Are you sure you want to go that route? It seems a bit impersonal. Did Jonas really have so much that you need an auction house to take care of it?"

Lucy interjected. "A lot of families choose to do that now, Aunt Tricia. Sometimes it's just too painful for those left behind to go through their loved ones' possessions."

Lenora nodded. "Yes, that's why I'm thinking it might have been a good idea to schedule an evaluation. Although the only things that Jonas had of any real value were his coin collection and some antique rifles, passed down from his grandfather."

She sighed. "I really can't bear the thought of looking through his things myself. At least, not yet."

Kira poked her head through the doorway. "Mother, should I bring your visitors some tea?"

Aunt Tricia looked at her friend, noting how tired she appeared, and waved away Kira's suggestion. "Oh, we really need to be going." She stood and Lucy followed suit.

They each embraced Mrs. Nelson again, reiterating that they were happy to help with anything that came up, before saying their goodbyes and following Kira down the hallway.

Dominic was in the foyer, clad in a long wool coat, and putting on his boots.

"How was she?" His tone was low, and his face showed his worry for his mother.

Aunt Tricia answered, speaking softly. "She'll be OK, Dominic. You all need to just pull together and get through this terrible tragedy as a family." Her tone was gentle and warm as she patted his back comfortingly. "We're here if you need us."

He nodded his thanks and opened the front door. "I was just going out. I'll walk you to your car."

The trio crunched through the snow together, and Lucy could tell there was something on the young man's mind. As they stopped at Lucy's SUV, he turned to face her.

"Has Taylor said anything to you about questioning Chad Prentiss?" His tone was hesitant, but his eyes locked on hers.

Lucy shook her head. "He's so busy with the investigation, I haven't seen him for more than a few minutes. What exactly happened, that your mother thinks Mr. Prentiss could be involved?"

Dominic was silent for a moment, seeming to carefully choose his words. "Jonas went to see Chad after our crops started to fail. I'm not sure what led my brother to believe this, or whether he had any proof, but he was convinced that Chad was dumping his wastewater from the tannery directly into the river. We use that water for our crops, you know."

Lucy nodded, frowning, as Dominic continued.

"Jonas came back all mussed up, with mud on the back of his coat. He said Chad got violent when he told him we were going to test our water, and that we're prepared to sue him, if his suspicion turns out to be true. He told me Chad shoved him and threatened to shoot him if he came on the property again."

Aunt Tricia gasped. "That's a bit extreme! Did Jonas call the police?"

Dominic shook his head. "I told him to, but he said he just needed to wait for that test result, and then he was going to sue the pants off Chad, and it wouldn't matter anymore. He'd lose his tannery."

Dominic looked grim. "I don't know if it was just a coincidence, that all this happened right before Jonas…" his voice caught, and he looked away, unable to continue. After a moment, he cleared his throat and said, "Anyway, I guess the police will get it all sorted out. But I'm mighty interested to know if Chad Prentiss has an alibi for that night."

Lucy and Aunt Tricia murmured their understanding, and Dominic gave a short nod.

"Thank you so much for coming by. It really means a lot to our family." He looked across the field, his eyes scanning the farm, and then stepped away from the car.

As they opened the doors to get in, he called out, "If either of you happen to see our dog, Ivan, please give me a call. He's been missing now for two nights."

11

"I have a small bit of good news!" Betsy announced, coming through the bakery door. "Joseph is going to take over as choral director for the children's Christmas concert!"

Lucy looked up from her recipe book and smiled. "That's wonderful news!"

"Amen to that," said Aunt Tricia. "This town needs something to look forward to."

"How's Mrs. Nelson holding up?" Betsy asked Lucy, her eyes worried. "Didn't you guys stop by there with food?"

"We did," Lucy confirmed. "She's having a tough time, as you can imagine." She briefly relayed the story that Dominic had told them about Jonas's trouble with the neighbor.

Betsy was shocked. "And that man had the nerve to show up on the Nelson's property the other night?"

Hannah looked up from where she was dusting lemon bars with powdered sugar. "You know, Lucy, even though Mrs.

Nelson seems to think Chad Prentiss may have been involved in Jonas's death, I've got to say... just the fact of him showing up there, the night of the murder, makes me think he didn't do it."

Lucy frowned, pondering Hannah's words. "Maybe. But also, it would be the best way to appear innocent, wouldn't it? Showing up right after the murder and asking what the commotion is about?"

"Hmm. Well, I suppose that's true," Hannah conceded.

"Are we officially calling it murder, then?" Aunt Tricia asked, looking over the tops of her spectacles.

Lucy shook her head. "I haven't heard anything since Taylor told us they'd ruled out a heart attack or stroke."

She glanced back at Betsy and Hannah. "By the way, while we were at Nelson Farm, Mrs. Nelson told us their dog Ivan is still missing. So, keep an eye out."

Betsy exclaimed, "Oh, that poor family! Haven't they been through enough?"

"I sure will," Hannah agreed. "I'll spread the word around town, too. Gosh, I remember how terrible it was when Spooky went missing." She set down the powdered sugar shaker and picked up the tray of pastries to carry out front. Going through the archway, she called over her shoulder, "Hey, Lucy, Taylor just pulled in!"

"Maybe he'll have some answers," Aunt Tricia commented, following Lucy out front. Betsy trailed behind.

The bell jangled as the deputy ducked through the doorway. "Good morning, ladies."

There was a chorus of greetings as Taylor approached the counter. Lucy looked into his face, thinking he looked weary and discouraged.

"Any progress?" she asked, pouring him a fresh cup of coffee. Aunt Tricia set a cinnamon roll in the microwave to heat it up and joined Lucy at the counter.

Taylor looked troubled as he spoke. "Jonas Nelson was poisoned. The coroner found strychnine in his system."

The ladies collectively gasped, exchanging glances. Hannah spoke first. "Could it have been an accident? I know they use strychnine in rat poison. They probably have to deal with rats over at the farm."

Taylor shook his head, his lips thinning. "I don't think so, as it wasn't inhaled. It was ingested. Mixed with food and eaten less than three hours before it killed him."

Lucy gulped, imagining what a horrible death that would have been. And to be alone in the snow when your body started to be affected… how terrible.

Aunt Tricia recovered her voice, though her fingers clutched at the cross around her neck. "What happens now, Taylor?"

The microwave dinged and Betsy retrieved Taylor's pastry, popping it into a cardboard clamshell, to go. She set it on the counter, and he nodded his thanks.

He met Aunt Tricia's gaze, answering her question. "We're going to search Jonas's house and vehicle and see if we can find the contaminated food."

Lucy voiced the question on all of their minds. "Does this mean it was definitely murder?" Her voice sounded hollow to her own ears.

Taylor sighed, picking up his coffee and pastry box. "It's sure starting to look that way. I've got to get back." He turned around and called back over his shoulder. "Thank you, ladies. Stay safe." His eyes zeroed in on Lucy. "I'll call you tonight, Lucy."

She nodded, and he walked out the door, passing another customer who was coming in.

The man was wearing a leather duster and a gray wool hat.

It took Lucy a second before she realized where she'd seen the man before, and when she did, her stomach dropped.

It was Chad Prentiss.

"Hello. May I help you?" Lucy strove to keep her voice normal, but her heartbeat thudded in her ears. *Was this Jonas's killer, right in front of her?*

"Good morning," Chad replied, turning his head to watch Taylor get into his cruiser. He turned back around. "Wasn't that Deputy Baker?"

Lucy nodded. She felt Hannah hovering at her elbow and knew she had recognized the man as well.

Chad frowned slightly and looked back at Lucy, searching her face. A moment later he snapped his fingers, startling her.

"Oh, that's right! I remember my sister telling me Deputy Baker is dating the owner of Sweet Delights Bakery. That must be you, right?" His blue eyes seemed cold and hard, not warm like Taylor's.

Lucy nodded mutely. She wished the man would state his business and leave.

Aunt Tricia spoke up. "Your sister?" It was obvious from her tone that she didn't care for Lucy to be the subject of gossip.

He waved a hand, irritated. "She's a hairdresser. One of her clients is the police department's dispatcher."

"Can we help you with something?" asked Betsy, after a quick glance at Aunt Tricia's and Lucy's faces.

The man ignored her question, turning his attention to Lucy alone.

"Have they found out anything about Jonas Nelson yet?" His eyes probed hers and Lucy felt uncomfortable. She cleared her throat.

"We haven't officially met. I'm Lucy Hale." She held out her hand, striving to be professional.

The man nodded but didn't accept her offered hand. "Chad Prentiss." He immediately returned to questioning Lucy. "Have they discovered the cause of death yet?"

Lucy shook her head, nonplussed. "I'm afraid you'd have to call the police department to find out."

Chad smirked. "Oh, come on. I'm sure you have the inside scoop if you're dating the deputy." He leaned forward, conspiratorially lowering his voice. "I can keep a secret."

Lucy frowned and stepped back. "I'm sorry, Mr. Prentiss. I have nothing to share."

The man stiffened at the reproach and his expression turned ugly. "Oh, I get it. You're friends with the Nelsons, right? You must have been brainwashed by all that nonsense they're spouting."

Aunt Tricia stepped forward, bristling at the mention of her grief-stricken friends.

"I'm afraid Sweet Delights Bakery has no wish for your patronage, Mr. Prentiss. Good day."

Her tone was dismissive and brooked no further comment. Fuming, Chad Prentiss stood glaring first at Aunt Tricia, with his narrowed eyes fixing on Lucy, next.

Without another word, he turned and left, the bell clanging loudly as he slammed the door.

12

"What is that you're making?" Hannah asked, peering at the assortment of wrapped baked goods stacked on top of the pastry case.

Lucy was rummaging through the cabinet under the counter, searching through the odds and ends they kept there.

Her voice was muffled as she replied. "A basket of treats to take to Heather Kelly, with our sympathies." She pulled her head out to look at Hannah quizzically.

"Have you seen the white wicker basket with the braided handle?"

Hannah nodded. "It's upstairs on the veranda, loaded down with spare silverware. Do you want me to go get it?"

Lucy shook her head, standing and dusting off her knees. "No, that's OK, thanks. I'll just use the mahogany basket we have in the storage room, though it's a little large."

Hannah nodded, then asked, "Do you want company? I'm all caught up out back."

Lucy smiled, pleasantly surprised. "Sure! That would be great. Let me get this together, and we can leave in about twenty minutes."

Lucy retrieved the basket from storage and arranged her selected items inside, adding a jar of local honey and a hand-appliquéd potholder from her vendor's displays. She scribbled a note to herself that she'd purchased those items, tucking the paper into the cash register.

Stepping back and eyeing the basket critically, she fashioned a looping bow out of some eggplant-purple silk ribbon, tying it to the handle. *There. Now it was perfect.*

A few minutes later, she and Hannah were pulling out of the parking lot, leaving Betsy and Aunt Tricia to mind the store. Heather Kelly lived on the south side of town, but not too far away. Lucy hoped to be back before the bakery closed.

They pulled into a concrete driveway adorned with large pots containing dwarf evergreens, decorated with tiny lights. The house was on the small side, a brown clapboard structure that Heather had inherited from her grandmother. Seeing the cheerful Christmas wreath hanging on the front door, Lucy was saddened by a sudden thought.

Jonas and Heather would never implement their plan of living in this house together after their nuptials, while they built a new house out on Nelson Farm.

She tucked the thought away, willing herself to keep a cheery face on for Heather's sake. She glanced at Hannah. "Ready?"

Hannah nodded, and the two made their way up the brick walkway, using the antique brass knocker to announce their presence.

Heather opened the door almost immediately. Her long hair was mussed, as if she had napped recently, and her eyes were red. But her face brightened when she saw Lucy and Hannah on her doorstep, her eyes lighting on the basket.

"Oh, how sweet of you." She stepped aside, opening the door wide. "Please, come in."

The girls followed Heather into a comfortable living room, done up in subdued tones of blue and green. The shades were drawn against the afternoon light, casting the room in deep shadow. Instead of opening the blinds, Heather chose to switch on a tabletop lamp.

"Have a seat, please," she indicated the couch, while taking a chair for herself.

Lucy and Heather sat down, setting the gift basket on the coffee table.

"How are you holding up?" Lucy asked, her voice soft with sympathy.

Heather looked away for a moment, then looked back, her eyes glistening. "It still doesn't seem real," she confessed, and then sighed. "I'm going over to Lenora's in a little while. I guess we're going to talk about… the arrangements." Heather took a deep breath. "I'm sure that will bring the truth home for me."

Lucy nodded, feeling so much compassion for the other woman, but helpless, as she couldn't think of anything encouraging to say.

"I'm sure just having you there will be a comfort to Mrs. Nelson," Hannah piped up, and Heather nodded with a sad smile.

"Yes, Lenora and I have always gotten along famously." Her tone was wistful. "I was so looking forward to her being my mother-in-law." Heather paused to compose herself, and then added, "I think both of us trying to save Jonas from his addiction is what really bonded us."

Lucy tilted her head quizzically. "What do you mean?"

Heather was silent for a moment, perhaps thinking she'd said too much, but then spoke up, her blue eyes meeting Lucy's questioning gaze.

"Ah, Jonas has had a gambling problem for a few years now," she confided. "But finally, when we got engaged, he was able to put that all behind him. He told me he was determined to make a fresh start."

Lucy was stunned. She'd known Jonas had run with a rough crowd as a teenager, and gotten into some scrapes in his early twenties, but she'd never heard a word about a gambling problem.

Hannah spoke up. "If you don't mind me asking… did Jonas owe money to anyone?" She hastened to add, afraid she'd overstepped, "Just thinking that if he did, you should make sure to tell Taylor. It might be important."

Heather nodded, her eyes clouded. "Hmm. I really don't know…" she hedged.

She bit her lip, finally admitting, "Mrs. Nelson had to take out another mortgage on the farm, you know, to pay off some of his debts. And Jonas felt so bad about that, especially now that the farm is on the verge of being repossessed."

She leaned forward, her expression becoming animated. "But Jonas had a plan to get them out of debt! He just told me recently."

Lucy raised her eyebrows, curious. "Really? What was that?"

Heather smoothed the fabric of her skirt over her knees. "Most people don't know this, but Jonas had a coin collection."

Lucy murmured, "Yes, I remember his mother mentioned that to me."

Heather nodded, her eyes widening. "He had one coin in particular—a 1943 copper wheat penny—that's super rare. He recently had it evaluated, and they told him it was worth a lot! I don't know how much, but Jonas said it would get the farm out of trouble."

Lucy sat back, stunned. *Could this be the motive for murder?*

Hannah had the same thought. "Heather, who else knew about this?"

Heather thought for a minute. "Just me and his family, I think. And I'm not even sure if they knew he'd taken it in to be evaluated."

Lucy spoke emphatically. "Heather, you absolutely *must* tell Taylor about this."

Heather nodded with a sigh. "I will." She looked away, gazing out the window, and Lucy could see her despair.

"We should probably get going," Hannah ventured, and Lucy agreed, rising to her feet.

"Thank you so much, ladies, for the gift basket," Heather said, following them out to the door. "It was very thoughtful of you."

They said their goodbyes, and Lucy and Hannah got into the SUV, watching as Heather shut the door. The light in the living room went out a minute later.

Lucy looked at Hannah, seeing her thoughts mirrored on her friend's face.

"A coin that valuable would be motive enough for murder, in some people's minds," Hannah said, her brow furrowed. "I sure hope she tells Taylor."

Lucy backed out of the driveway. "I hate to interfere, but I think I might mention it to Taylor myself."

"Wouldn't hurt," Hannah agreed.

Lucy's phone buzzed in her purse, and she fished it out, one-handed.

"Speak of the devil," she murmured to Hannah. She pressed the connect button and said, "Hello? Taylor?"

Taylor's voice was grim. "Lucy, I have some news."

Lucy gripped the receiver. "What? What's wrong?" She could tell he was upset by something. She could hear voices in the background. "Where are you?"

"I'm at the lab. We've just come from Jonas Nelson's house." The voices in the background lessened, as though he'd walked to a quieter corner.

"Lucy, we found the poisoned food Jonas ate, right there on his kitchen counter."

"What was it?" Lucy asked, her heart pounding. She knew something was terribly, terribly wrong, just from Taylor's terse tone.

"It was fruitcake, Lucy. Fruitcake in a cellophane package with your bakery's logo on it."

13

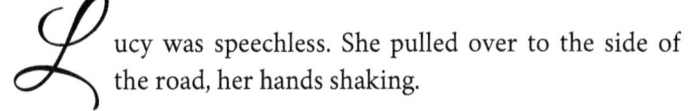

Lucy was speechless. She pulled over to the side of the road, her hands shaking.

"How... how could that be?" she asked, her head swimming. *Poison? In a Sweet Delights Bakery fruitcake?*

"What is it?" Hannah whispered, tugging at Lucy's sleeve. Lucy glanced at her friend's worried face, and requested, "Taylor, is it OK if I put you on speakerphone? Hannah's with me."

At his agreement, Lucy punched the button, and the deputy's voice soon filled the car.

"I just told Lucy we found a fruitcake in Jonas's house, poisoned with strychnine. It was still wrapped in Sweet Delights Bakery's packaging, with one slice taken out."

Hannah's jaw dropped. "I don't understand," she whispered. "You're saying there was poison in one of our cakes?" She looked at Lucy, her eyes wide. "But those cakes are for sale at Bing's Grocery right now!"

Lucy looked stricken. "Taylor, we need to pull all of those cakes! Or could there be strychnine in our raw ingredients? Do we have to worry that our flour or sugar is contaminated?"

She felt sick at the thought of the town's residents, enjoying her products, suddenly becoming ill, or worse.

Hannah fished out her phone. "I need to call the bakery!" she announced, in a near panic. Her eyebrows shot up. "Or should we call Bing's first?"

Taylor heard their frazzled voices and cut in, his tone firm. "Ladies, let's not get ahead of ourselves. We've not had any reports of people getting sick from eating the bakery's products. I suspect the poisoning was done after the cake was purchased. Lucy, did Jonas or Mrs. Nelson buy a fruitcake from the bakery?"

Lucy shook her head. "No, not that I know of." Her thoughts were scrambled, and she was having a hard time processing the situation. The Nelsons didn't usually patronize the bakery–Lenora Nelson was a great baker in her own right.

Taylor said, "OK. Lucy, here's what I want you to do. Stop by Bing's Grocery and pick up one of your cakes and then bring it down to the station."

Lucy took a deep breath, still feeling unnerved. "OK. I will. I'll be there in a few minutes."

She hung up and looked at Hannah. "Can I drop you off at the bakery first, so you can tell Aunt Tricia and Betsy what's going on? But tell them not to panic. We don't really know anything yet."

Hannah nodded, her usual rosy complexion looking pallid. "Sure."

A few minutes later, Lucy was again pulling out of the parking lot, headed for Bing's Grocery, leaving Hannah behind. As she entered Bing's, she wondered what she would say if someone questioned why she was buying one of her own cakes.

"I'll cross that bridge when I come to it," she mumbled to herself, earning a strange look from an older woman as she passed by.

Thankfully, the cashier was too distracted to even notice who Lucy was, and she was soon back in her car, zipping over to the police department. She eyed the cellophane packaged cake on the seat beside her, knowing she'd never look at fruitcakes with nostalgic joy again.

When she entered the police station, she saw Taylor immediately, standing by the doorway to his office. He must have been watching for her. She rushed over to him, and he ushered her into into his office.

The offending fruitcake was sitting on his desk, or what was left of it. It had been chopped into sections. Lucy supposed that was so they could send chunks of it to the lab.

Her heart sank as she recognized the slight green tint of the cellophane she always used and spotted the trademark pink and black label with Sweet Delights Bakery's logo.

She set the cake from Bing's Grocery down beside it, and stepped back, her eyes drifting back and forth between the two.

She immediately noticed the differences and got excited, pointing her finger at the poisoned fruitcake.

"Taylor, that cake isn't from Sweet Delights Bakery! Someone just used our packaging. Look, see the fluted sides? The ridges? We don't use pans like that. Our tube pans have straight sides. I find fluted pans cause cakes to stick."

Taylor bent his head to inspect the contaminated cake, and Lucy bent beside him, peering closely at the cut sections.

"Ah! Look there. See the green candied cherries? Also, not something we use. Hannah hates green candied cherries. Even though Mom's old recipe included them, our new recipe this year only has red cherries, and pineapple and dates."

She straightened up, thoroughly relieved. "That's not our fruitcake, Taylor. I can swear to it."

Taylor straightened, too, looking thoughtful. "I believe you, Lucy. Of course, I'll still send samples of your cake out to the lab, but the differences are obvious, even to the naked eye."

Lucy folded her arms, hugging herself. She was relieved to be exonerated, but still felt alarmed. Someone had used—probably re-used, she realized—Sweet Delights Bakery's packaging, to try and pin the murder on her!

"Who would do that?" she whispered, growing cold at the thought. "Poison Jonas and make it look like it was my product?"

Taylor wrapped an arm around her shoulders, giving her a squeeze. "I don't know, Lucy. But I promise you, we will find out."

Lucy stared down at the offending cake. "So, this was in Jonas's mobile home?"

Taylor nodded. "Right there on his kitchen counter, with only a single slice gone."

Lucy frowned. "Is the strychnine that strong? That one slice was all it took?"

Taylor's expression was grave. "The lab said the amount of strychnine in the piece they analyzed was enough to kill a grown man within hours. The thing about strychnine is, when it's in something with a strong flavor of its own, you can't even taste it."

Lucy's eyes clouded. "Poor Jonas! He must have had some right before his shift at the Christmas tree stand."

She looked up at Taylor as she realized something. "Did you tell Mrs. Nelson, yet? Maybe she'll know where Jonas got the fruitcake."

Taylor shook his head. "Honestly, Lucy, I just wanted to clear your name before we did anything else here." His caring expression softened Lucy's heart. He always was looking out for her.

"Thank you for that," she said, rising on her toes to kiss his cheek. "Any other clues come up?"

Taylor rested his hip on the corner of the desk, running a hand through his hair. It was a habit Lucy had witnessed before when he was frustrated about a case.

"Honestly, Lucy, I can't imagine who would hate Jonas enough to kill him. We're still planning to pull Al Forrester in for questioning, but I have my doubts that it was him. I just issued the man a warning a day before the murder, telling him he needed to let Heather go, or wind up behind bars. This would be a bold move, right on the heels of that."

Something tickled at Lucy's brain; something she'd been thinking Taylor should know. Suddenly, it came to her.

"Taylor, I think Jonas was avoiding someone... someone he may have borrowed money from. And I'm pretty sure Hannah and I saw the man, ourselves, right here in Ivy Creek."

14

Taylor frowned. "What are you talking about? Why would Jonas borrow money? For the farm?"

Lucy shook her head. "I don't think so. Heather Kelly told me Jonas had a gambling problem, but he was trying to get past it. She indicated that's why the farm is in trouble."

Taylor looked sober. "I never knew that. Jonas had some troubles years ago, running with a rough crowd, but I thought he'd been on a straight and narrow path for some time."

"He has been," Lucy insisted. "Heather said ever since they were engaged, he'd sworn off gambling. But it's possible he still had some old debts. And with the farm doing so poorly, I doubt he was able to pay them off."

Taylor scratched his head. "You'll have to back up here. What makes you think Jonas was avoiding someone? Who did you and Hannah see?"

Lucy recounted what they'd witnessed outside the tavern, ending with the stranger's message, "Tell your pal Jonas that Vic is looking for him."

Taylor stood up from the desk with a low whistle. "That description sounds an awful lot like Vic D'Angelo."

"Who's that?" Lucy could tell from the expression on Taylor's face that the man was dangerous.

Taylor explained, "Vic is supposedly one of the henchmen for the crime syndicate in Lowell. The cops have never been able to pin anything on him, but there are reports he's involved with drugs, gambling, maybe even prostitution. He's been arrested for assault in several cases, in conjunction with Marco Spinelli, a suspected loan shark."

Lucy was horrified. "Do you think Vic might have killed Jonas because he owed Spinelli money?"

Taylor paced the room, thinking out loud. "That doesn't really make sense. Dead men can't pay their debts. Unless…" He sat down at his desk and tapped a few keys, booting up his computer.

"What is it?" Lucy asked, coming to stand behind him.

Taylor scrolled through pages, searching for something. "Here. There was a raid in Lowell a few months ago, arresting several individuals thought to be involved in illegal gambling. The break in the case came from an anonymous tip." He looked up at Lucy.

"They kept most of the details out of the press, but I'll make a few phone calls. I have a buddy on the force over in Lowell."

Lucy was puzzled. "What's the connection? As you said, dead men don't pay their debts."

Taylor drummed his fingers on the desk. "They don't. But what if Jonas was the source of the anonymous tip? It could be a revenge killing."

Lucy pondered that idea. It was certainly possible. She saw Taylor was itching to investigate, so she decided to be on her way.

"Let me know what you find out," she said, bending to kiss his cheek.

"I will," he said. He met her gaze. "Be careful, Lucy."

"Always." She gave him a smile as she left his office.

Once back in her car, she mulled over what she had learned. *Could Jonas's murder be a revenge killing?* She wasn't so sure about that.

Even though Taylor doubted that Al Forrester, Heather's ex-husband, was involved, Lucy still had a bad feeling about him. A lot of murders were committed by spurned romantic partners, after all.

She suddenly remembered what she had learned from Heather about the valuable coin Jonas had. She started to go back inside to share that info with Taylor, but stopped, her hand on the car door latch. She decided she'd give him a chance to find out what he could from his friend on the Lowell police force–knowing Taylor, he'd called the man the minute she'd left. She'd call him later, from the bakery.

As she began her journey back to the bakery, Lucy decided to drive through the north side of town, where a lot of new shops had opened up. Her brain needed time to process all that had happened, and so far, she'd had no luck finding a vintage ceramic tree for Aunt Tricia's present, though she'd looked online several times. She might have to think of another gift, and time was running out.

She drove slowly, trying to cheer herself by looking at the various Christmas decorations decorating the shop fronts. One particularly elaborate display was on the roof of the local hardware store, featuring Santa in his sleigh, pulled by nine reindeer, the first one in line sporting a glowing red nose.

She passed by a small town square, where a manger scene had been set up in the center. Statues of the three wise men surrounded the three-sided miniature structure, inside of which the baby Jesus lay in a cradle, under the loving gaze of Mary and Joseph. Soft yellow spotlights gave the scene an ethereal glow, and the snow blanketing the ground set it off perfectly.

So enraptured was Lucy by the magical scene, she almost drove right past a new shop with an intriguing name: Cleo's Collectibles. She slowed down, taking a look.

It was an antique store, and Lucy felt a stirring of excitement. She loved browsing antique stores any time of year. And now, at Christmas, she thought an antique store may yield the perfect present for Aunt Tricia, whether it be an Atlantic ceramic tree or something else. Her aunt was very fond of vintage items.

Parking was unavailable right in front, as Cleo's Collectibles was sandwiched between a card shop and an alley, with a music store on the alley's other side. Both the music store and the card shop seemed to be doing a brisk business.

Lucy finally found a spot just past the music store and decided that was the best she was going to get. *A little walking never hurt anyone.*

She zipped up her jacket again, as the afternoon had gotten chillier. As she passed the alley, she glanced down its length and saw something moving in the shadows.

Squinting into the dark passageway, she realized it was a dog, picking through what looked to be a trash bag. Her heart went out to the poor animal, living on the streets. She'd never been afraid of dogs, so she stopped, crouching, holding out one gloved hand.

"Hey, there," she said softly, and the animal looked up, approaching cautiously. It was about fifteen feet away now, and though it was still in the shadows, she saw it wag its tail hopefully. "It's OK. I won't hurt you."

Poor thing was probably hungry, she thought, wondering if there was a sandwich shop nearby. The least she could do was provide it with a decent meal. After all, it was Christmastime.

The dog came further into the light, and Lucy's eyes widened. She wasn't entirely sure, but it looked like it might be Ivan, the Nelson's dog.

"Ivan?" she called. "Is that you, boy?"

15

The dog stopped and looked at Lucy, tilting its head.

Maybe it *was* Ivan, Lucy thought, with a rush of excitement. She'd only met the farm's dog a few times, so she couldn't be sure… but how wonderful it would be if she could bring Lenora Nelson's lost dog home to her!

"C'mon, Ivan," she encouraged. "Do you want to go home?"

At the word "home", the dog's ears pricked up, and he began to cautiously come forward again.

Just then, a car door slammed on the street, startling the animal. He flinched, and bolted, running away, leaving Lucy sorely disappointed. She straightened up with a sigh and then pulled out her phone.

Since she didn't know for sure if it was Ivan, it would be silly to chase the dog down the alley. She'd call the Nelson's house and mention she might have spotted him. The answering system picked up after a few rings, and Dominic's voice came over the line. Lucy waited for the beep, and left a brief message, including the name of the cross street nearby.

She ended her call and glanced down the alley again, but the dog hadn't reappeared. *Maybe it would be there again when she came out of the antique shop.*

She mentally crossed her fingers and walked on, soon coming to the door of Cleo's Collectibles. She stopped for a moment in the street, admiring the front window display.

An antique rocking chair held a large wooden Nutcracker soldier standing several feet tall. An antique checkerboard constructed of light and dark wood was set up on a small table in front of him. His would-be opponent, a large plush toy fashioned after Rudolph the red-nosed reindeer, sat in another rocking chair, his four legs akimbo. A white artificial Christmas tree was behind them, its tiny lights twinkling.

Seeing the white tree, a true blast from the past, gave Lucy fresh hope that the store might yield the vintage ceramic tree she was looking for. She opened the door and stepped inside.

The store was dimly lit, and Lucy blinked, her eyes adjusting from the brightness outdoors. There were no overhead lights on, she noticed. Instead, at least a dozen floor and table lamps, all tagged for sale, were lit up. They emitted varying degrees and shades of illumination, lending a warm and cozy ambience to the shop.

The homey atmosphere was completed by the presence of a large, striped, orange and white cat, who came to greet Lucy immediately, winding around her ankles.

Lucy smiled and bent down to stroke the feline's head. "Well, hello there," she murmured. "Aren't you the friendly one?"

A woman's voice came from the far side of the shop. "That's Cleo," she said. "She's welcoming you to her shop." The obvious affection in the proprietor's voice had Lucy realizing she'd found a kindred spirit: a cat person.

Lucy grinned at the woman and walked forward, with Cleo zig-zagging in front of her.

"Hello," Lucy held out her hand. "I'm Lucy Hale."

The woman shook her hand with a surprisingly firm grip. "Rosalyn Sykes," she said, her green eyes full of good humor. "I'm pleased to meet you."

Rosalyn looked to be in her fifties and had a halo of soft blonde curls framing a round face with dimples. She wore a festive Christmas sweater featuring gnomes. Her fingers were adorned with multiple rings, and a chunky amethyst pendant hung low on her chest. She peered over the counter at Cleo, who now seemed obsessed with Lucy's shoes.

Lucy looked down, commenting, "Cleo must have picked up Gigi's scent. That's my Persian."

Rosalyn made a clucking sound and Cleo looked up inquisitively. "Don't be rude, Cleo. Come sit in your chair."

Rosalyn patted a padded captain's chair behind the counter, and Cleo looked up, meowing. Lucy watched the feline skirt the base of the counter, moments later hopping into the chair. She settled down with a rumbling purr, looking pleased with herself, her eyes no more than slits.

Lucy chuckled. "So, Cleo has her own throne. My Gigi would be jealous." She glanced around the store admiringly and then back at Rosalyn, saying, "What a lovely shop you have!"

"Why, thank you," Rosalyn beamed. "A little bit of everything, I always say. You never know what you'll find."

Lucy looked speculative. "I don't suppose you've come across any Atlantic mold ceramic Christmas trees?"

Rosalyn pursed her lips, thinking. "What decade are you looking for? They began production in 1958 but didn't become really popular until the '70s."

Lucy opened her mouth to answer but was suddenly interrupted by a man coming through the closed door, located behind the counter.

"Oh, hello," Lucy said.

The man nodded at her with a quick hello before turning to Rosalyn. "I'm off to look at that jukebox, then," he said, without preamble. He was tall and thin, with angular face, and looked to be Lucy's own age, or perhaps a bit older.

Rosalyn nodded, saying to Lucy, "Excuse me for one minute."

She stepped over to the cash register and opened it, removing the cash drawer to retrieve a check from underneath. She addressed the two of them over her shoulder, "Oh, by the way, Lucy, this is Drew, my nephew."

"Drew, Lucy's looking for an Atlantic ceramic tree from..." She closed the register and stepped back over, handing Drew a check. She asked Lucy, "What decade did you say?"

"1970's," Lucy answered, adding, "I'm not sure the exact year. I'm trying to replace one for my aunt, and I can describe it, if you'd like."

Rosalyn nodded and grabbed a notepad. "Yes, please do. I'm sure we don't have any from that period at the moment, but we can be on the lookout and give you a call."

Lucy closed her eyes, recalling all the details she could, and Rosalyn jotted them down.

Drew stood silently until she was done, and then looked at his watch. "I've got to be going," he said. "It was nice meeting you, Lucy." He turned and left, exiting through the door behind the counter.

Rosalyn called out, "Good luck!" She turned back to Lucy. "Well, it will be a good day, indeed, if he can make a deal for that jukebox. Drew's on a bit of a downswing right now. He could use a win."

Lucy nodded politely, not knowing how to respond. Rosalyn chatted on, as though she and Lucy were old friends.

"Drew's my sister Anna's boy," she confided. "One of those young men who never figured out what he wanted to do with his life. Anna finally lost patience with him last September, and booted him out, telling him to go find himself."

Rosalyn laughed at Lucy's look of surprise. "Well, he needed that kick in the pants, actually. Decided he needed a fresh start, and next thing you know, he's come clear across the country, knocking on my door. But blood's blood, and since I don't have any kids myself–"

She stopped to tickle Cleo under the chin. "Except for this one, of course. Anyway, I told Drew he could live in the efficiency apartment back there." She jabbed her thumb at the door behind her.

"He wants to learn the antique trade, so I'll give him a year and then we'll see where we're at. After all, I'm not going to be around forever. It's a nice thought that Cleo's Collectibles will keep going, after I'm gone." She sighed, apparently finished, and looked at Lucy expectantly.

It had been quite a disclosure, and Lucy was a bit nonplussed. She cast about for something to say, remembering the dog in the alleyway.

"Say, Rosalyn, when I came in, I spotted a large black dog in the alley. I think he might belong to a friend of mine who lost hers. Have you seen him?"

Rosalyn nodded. "He's only been hanging around for a few days. Drew wanted to call the dog pound, but I think that's jumping the gun. I gave the poor thing some bacon the other day. Nice dog, but rather skittish."

Lucy got excited. "Only for a few days? That fits the timeline of when he went . He got spooked when I was trying to get close to him, but I called the owner and left a message. They'll probably come around soon."

Rosalyn nodded. "That would be good. Winter around here is not kind to stray animals."

Lucy agreed. She looked at her watch. "Well, I need to get going. I'll take a look as I leave. Maybe he's back in the alley."

She smiled at Rosalyn, and then at Cleo, sitting so contentedly, the queen of her domain.

"It was a pleasure to meet you, Rosalyn. Please give me a call if you come across one of those ceramic trees." Lucy fished her business card out of her purse, handing it over.

Rosalyn glanced down, her eyes widening. "Sweet Delights Bakery! Wow, my friend was just telling me they carry your fruitcakes over at Bing's Grocery now."

Lucy's smile froze on her face at the mention of fruitcake, but Rosalyn didn't notice, thanking her for coming in.

They said their goodbyes, and Lucy let herself out of the shop, glancing at the darkening sky before hurrying over to the alley to peer down into the shadows. The dog was nowhere to be seen.

Maybe that means Dominic already came and picked Ivan up, she thought hopefully, getting into her car and starting it up.

She sure hoped so. The Nelsons could use a Christmas miracle right about now.

16

*L*ucy sighed, hanging up the bakery phone. Dominic Nelson had called first thing this morning, but he didn't have good news. When he'd gone over to the alley near the antique shop last evening, the dog Lucy had seen was nowhere in sight. He told her he'd gone back again this morning, but still no luck. She promised him she'd keep a lookout.

"What's up?" asked Hannah, who was replenishing a tray of espresso brownies in the pastry case.

Lucy filled her in on what Dominic had said, and Hannah's face fell.

"Oh, man. I really thought Ivan would be home this morning, after you told me you'd seen him yesterday."

Lucy nodded. "Me, too. But I don't know for sure that dog was even Ivan. Maybe it was just a stray black dog."

Hannah nodded and sighed, saying wistfully, "If I could, I'd adopt all the strays out there. It doesn't seem right for animals to have to live on the street."

Lucy smiled at her friend's soft-hearted nature. "Spooky would never forgive you if you adopted a dog."

Hannah chuckled. "Neither would my landlord."

The bell jangled, and Betsy breezed in, a jovial look on her face.

"Look who's here!" she called out gaily, gesturing to the parking lot. "Joseph brought in his choir students for a treat before they begin their rehearsal!"

Lucy raised her eyebrows, seeing the group of children disembarking from two white vans in the parking lot. "That's... ambitious," she commented. The group of fifteen kids, all primary school age, looked pretty rowdy.

Hannah asked Betsy, "Who's the other adult? I don't recognize him."

Betsy hung up her coat and came around the counter, tying on an apron. "That's Joseph's new theater assistant, Miles."

Lucy sidled a look at Hannah. It appeared the young man had captured her attention. He looked to be around the same age as she and Hannah, and was a pleasant-looking fellow, tall and red-headed, wearing a navy peacoat.

The bell jangled and Joseph came in first, grinning at Lucy as he held the door open for all the children. "Hello! I hope you have plenty of treats in stock. I've promised the kids one each of their choosing, before we begin today's rehearsal." His eyes twinkled. "In exchange for everyone's very best efforts today."

The children filed in, pushing and shoving each other as they crowded in front of the pastry case, their eyes wide at the array of sweets.

Miles stepped forward with a smile. He had a smattering of freckles and a complexion made ruddy by the chill outdoors. "Wow, it smells so good in here! Hi, I'm Miles. I'm new to town, and never even heard about your bakery until Joseph mentioned it today."

Lucy smiled. "Well, now that you know about us, I hope you'll come back. I'm Lucy." She held out her hand and Miles shook it. Lucy gestured to Hannah. "This is Hannah, who does most of the baking."

Miles looked at Hannah with admiration. "Hi, Hannah," he said, his green eyes intent on her face. "I'm pleased to meet you."

Hannah blinked, a blush rising on her cheeks. "Hi," she mumbled. She turned to Lucy. "I've got to go check the oven." She turned and walked away, leaving Miles staring after her with a puzzled expression.

Lucy tried to think of something to say in the awkward moment that followed, but just then, a quibble among two boys broke out, and her attention was distracted.

"I said I wanted it first!"

"No, you didn't, and even if you had, I'm older than you, so I get to choose first!"

"Who says? I was first in the door, and I called dibs!"

Joseph looked over at the boys as he accepted a coffee from Betsy. "What are we debating about, fellas?"

He walked over to see what had caused the uproar. A single coconut macaroon brownie sat on a tray inside the case, apparently coveted by two boys who looked to be about ten years old.

Joseph looked at Lucy. "Got any more of those in the back?"

Lucy shook her head. "Sorry, no. Mrs. White came in a few hours ago and bought a dozen."

Joseph pursed his lips for a moment, then suggested, "How about you guys do a rock-paper-scissors for it? That seems fair."

The boys jumped on the idea; the argument forgotten with the opportunity to compete.

"Best of three gets it?" suggested one boy, and the other nodded. Soon they were embroiled in the game, and a winner was declared.

"Nice save," Lucy congratulated Joseph with amusement as he walked over to the counter.

He grinned. "Lessons learned growing up with brothers." He pulled out his wallet as the boys began ordering their treats. Betsy bagged each treat separately, handing them over to the children while Lucy rang them all in, giving Joseph a discount.

Within ten minutes, the troop was exiting the bakery, with Miles leading the way and Joseph bringing up the rear.

The bell jangled once more, and the bakery felt strangely empty in the children's absence.

"Joseph is so great with children," Betsy sighed, dreamy-eyed.

Lucy hid her smile. She could see wedding bells in the couple's future. The thought of romance had her remembering Hannah's strange reaction to Miles.

If she knew her friend at all, she'd say Hannah was attracted to the man, and just too tongue-tied to think of anything to say. Lucy itched to do a little matchmaking between the two but resisted the urge. It was best to just let things progress as they would.

The morning passed by with Lucy dividing her time between helping Hannah with the baking and assisting Betsy at the front counter. Aunt Tricia had finally been convinced to take a day off.

Just after the lunch rush, Lucy was decorating some Christmas cupcakes in the kitchen when Betsy poked her head through the archway.

"Lucy, Mrs. Nelson just came in." Betsy's eyes were wide. "She brought in a huge box of dog cookies to sell!"

Lucy hurriedly washed her hands, taking off her apron and hanging it up. She hadn't expected Mrs. Nelson to proceed with her plans to be a vendor yet, with Jonas's death still so recent.

She went through the archway and saw Mrs. Nelson standing in the center of the front room. A cardboard box was set on the café table in front of her.

Lucy rounded the counter, walking over with a smile. "Mrs. Nelson! What a nice surprise." The grieving mother's face looked tired and drawn, but her eyes smiled as Lucy approached.

"Hi, Lucy. I hope you don't mind that I went ahead and brought these in now." She twisted her hands restlessly, her dark eyes stark in her pale face. "I just don't know what to do with myself, so I've been making more dog biscuits." She looked around the room. "Is your aunt here today?"

Lucy shook her head. "She has the day off. No, of course I don't mind. I had already prepared a space for you, right after the first time we spoke about it."

She gestured to a chair. "Please, sit. Let me get you a cup of coffee and we'll chat for a minute."

Mrs. Nelson protested, "Oh, no, I know you're busy. I don't want to keep you from your work."

Lucy insisted, knowing Aunt Tricia would ask questions about how her friend was holding up. "No, I'm due a break, anyway. Just for a few minutes, OK?"

Mrs. Nelson nodded, pulling out a chair and settling into it, as Lucy fetched them both a coffee. On impulse, she added a few shortbread cookies to a plate, and brought everything over with Betsy's help.

Mrs. Nelson took a sip and closed her eyes, savoring it. She opened them and said with a wan smile, "You always have the best coffee. Thank you, dear."

Lucy smiled. "Please, have a cookie." She inquired gently, "Any news on the investigation?"

Mrs. Nelson shook her head. "No. But Taylor called me about Joseph's coin collection. He said Heather had told him Joseph had a 1943 copper wheat penny. I don't know anything about coins, but apparently that one is very valuable."

Lucy sighed with relief. She was glad Heather had called Taylor with that information.

"What did Taylor say?"

Mrs. Nelson looked troubled. "He asked me to verify that the collection was still in Joseph's house. You know, I haven't been in there at all since…" her voice trailed off.

Lucy nodded sympathetically. "I'm so sorry. Maybe Dominic could do that for you."

The other woman shook her head. "Maybe I should have asked him, but I already went in there myself." She drew a ragged breath, and Lucy could see she was hanging on to her composure by a thread.

Lucy reached out and squeezed her hand. "Was it there?"

Mrs. Nelson looked at her, her face distraught. "Lucy, I can't say for sure, but I think the house has been ransacked. I can't believe Jonas would have kept it in such a mess, since Heather would often visit him."

Lucy was shocked. "Ransacked? Did you tell Taylor? Was the coin collection missing?"

Mrs. Nelson's voice quavered as she answered, "I reported a possible break-in immediately. Although, I found the coin album in a cabinet in the living room."

Lucy sighed in relief. "OK. That's good then. Maybe Jonas had been too busy with Christmas to tidy up."

Mrs. Nelson shook her head, her eyes troubled. "I don't think so, Lucy. The coin collection was there, but the slot for the copper wheat penny was empty."

17

Lucy's hand flew to her mouth. "Oh, no! Did you report it missing?"

The other woman nodded, but added, "As I explained to Taylor, it's quite possible Jonas hid the coin for safe keeping. The police have cordoned off Jonas's house now, and I guess they'll be dusting for fingerprints." She sighed, a tremulous sound, and fiddled with her coffee cup.

Looking up at Lucy, she said, "All of this is really too much. I can't sleep at night, thinking someone may have broken into Jonas's house… that maybe the person who murdered my son was right there again, on my property." She looked away, adding morosely, "And Ivan is still missing."

Lucy's heart sank. "I was really hoping that Dominic would find him near that antique shop. But, honestly, I'm not even sure it was Ivan I saw." Her heart went out to the Nelson family, with so much trouble and grief on their plate. She wished there was something else she could do.

Mrs. Nelson sipped her coffee, and suddenly sat taller, straightening her spine. "Well, there's nothing to be done about any of that, so I need to focus on what I can control." Her eyes met Lucy's, now full of determination. "Did you say you have a table for my dog cookies? I think setting that up will be a nice distraction."

Lucy nodded, rising to her feet. This, at least, was something she could help with. "Yes, let me go get the table. I'll be back in a jiffy."

As she left the room, she tried to shrug off the lingering sadness she felt, reminding herself that Mrs. Nelson needed those around her to be strong and filled with positive energy.

Aunt Tricia shook her head and sighed. "If only Taylor could catch a break in the case before Christmas."

She was sitting at the kitchen table with Lucy, who had just filled her in on the visit with Mrs. Nelson.

Lucy nodded, drumming her fingers on the table. "Or even if Ivan could be found by then. The Nelsons need something good to happen."

"Did anything ever come of Taylor questioning Heather's fiancé?" Aunt Tricia nibbled on a Christmas cookie.

When Lucy had come home, she'd found Aunt Tricia had been busy on her day off. There was a fresh plate of cream cheese spritz cookies on the table, shaped into little green trees. Why her aunt would bake at home when she had the bakery at her disposal was a mystery to Lucy, but she suspected it was a nostalgic exercise.

Lucy frowned. "Taylor said he questioned Al, but apparently, he had an alibi. Although it was an iffy one. He said he'd been at a restaurant, and then taken a drive. So, who's to say where he actually went after the restaurant."

"And what about that neighbor of Lenora's?" asked Aunt Tricia, her face darkening. It was clear she didn't care much for Chad Prentiss.

Lucy shook her head. "I don't know, Auntie. Taylor's been so busy, I hardly get to speak to him on the phone for more than a minute at a time." She picked up a cookie and bit into it, consoling herself with the sweet. Truth be told, she missed Taylor. She'd had visions of this Christmas being extra special, now that they'd begun dating again.

Lucy rose from the table, pushing away those thoughts. Taylor was doing exactly what he needed to do, and she'd have plenty of time with him once the case was solved.

"I think I'll go take a bubble bath," she told her aunt, picking up her teacup.

Aunt Tricia looked mildly alarmed, glancing at the clock and then back at Lucy. "Why don't you wait a few more minutes, dear? I haven't seen you all day."

The request seemed strange to Lucy. She and Aunt Tricia shared a house, after all. But she knew her aunt had been feeling a bit low, so she immediately settled back into her chair.

"OK. I'm not in a rush." She looked at Aunt Tricia, wondering what was going through her mind. "Um... how about we watch a Christmas movie later? Your choice."

Aunt Tricia smiled. "That might be nice." She glanced at the clock again, mystifying Lucy. *What was going on?*

Lucy opened her mouth to question her, but just then the doorbell rang. Aunt Tricia's face broke into a secretive smile, but she remained seated.

"Why don't you get that, dear," she suggested to Lucy, mischief twinkling in her eyes.

With a funny look at Aunt Tricia, Lucy nodded, heading into the living room. She crossed to the door, peeking out the window at the driveway. *It was Taylor! What a nice surprise.*

She chuckled as she twisted the doorknob. The reason behind Aunt Tricia's baking project was now clear.

"Hello–" Lucy's greeting was cut short as she swung open the door. She was expecting her favorite fella, but the sight before her had her mouth dropping open in surprise.

A massive Fraser fir tree was standing on the front porch, and Taylor's face peeked around the side, with a boyish grin on his face.

"Surprise!"

Lucy grinned at him, delighted. "Oh, Taylor! How wonderful! Are you able to stay and decorate it with me?"

He nodded, pleased with her joyful reaction. "Barring any emergency, I officially have the evening off." Lucy squealed and planted a kiss on his cheek, her evening now completely turned around.

Aunt Tricia said from the doorway, "Well, let the man in, Lucy!" Her face had the expression of the cat who ate the canary, and Lucy squeezed her arm affectionately.

Together, they wrangled the huge evergreen into the living room, and Aunt Tricia took the tree stand out of the closet.

She watched as Taylor set up the tree, and she and Lucy instructed him on which side looked best.

The three of them stepped back together, admiring the magnificent fir tree.

"Where did you get it?" Lucy asked. She knew the Nelson Farm Christmas Tree stand was still closed.

"I went over to Gilead right after work." Taylor chuckled, taking in the size of the tree. "I sure hope you ladies have enough ornaments for this beast."

Lucy grinned and scooted off to retrieve the boxes she and Aunt Tricia had taken down from the attic, while her aunt ducked into the kitchen to get refreshments.

"Cider and cookies coming up," Aunt Tricia called.

Twenty minutes later, Nat King Cole was playing on the stereo, and the tree was looking quite festive, hung with garland and light strings, and dozens of vintage ornaments.

Lucy looked at Taylor, holding up the multi-faceted gold star she'd saved for last. "Will you do the honors?"

Taylor looked pleased and accepted the star, reaching up high to place it with care on the very top. He stepped back, and Lucy plugged in the lights, holding her breath that no bulbs were out.

They all lit up perfectly, and she smiled, a rush of Christmas nostalgia warming her. With all the trouble going on, it had been easy to lose sight of how wonderful the holiday season was.

Suddenly, Taylor's phone rang, and he pulled it from his pocket, looking down at it with a frown. "Excuse me," he said, stepping into the dining room.

Lucy's warm and fuzzy feeling ebbed away as she caught the clipped tones of his conversation. She and Aunt Tricia exchanged looks. Whatever was going on, it sounded important.

Taylor reappeared, his face sober. "I'm sorry, ladies. I need to go into the station."

Lucy nodded, resolving to just be glad they'd spent a little time together.

"What happened?" Aunt Tricia asked, her eyes worried.

Taylor's lips compressed. "They picked up Vic D'Angelo on the outskirts of town, with a taillight out. He was acting in a suspicious manner, so the officer searched his car."

Lucy's eyes widened. "What did they find?"

Taylor's tone was grim. "There was a gas station receipt from the night Jonas was murdered, from a station only a block away from Nelson Farm."

18

"He's being held for questioning." Taylor dropped a kiss on Lucy's forehead. "I want to talk to him myself. Sorry I have to cut our evening short…"

Lucy waved away his apology, her head swimming with the implications. *This could be the break they needed in the case!*

"It's fine," she mustered up a smile for him. "Thank you for bringing the tree! I'm so glad we got to decorate it together." She walked him to the door, and Aunt Tricia added her goodbyes as Taylor opened the door and headed for his car.

Lucy shut the door and looked at Aunt Tricia, hope in her eyes. "Maybe this will all be wrapped up soon, and the Nelson family can get some closure."

"From your lips to God's ears," Aunt Tricia murmured, starting to gather up the empty boxes from the room.

"So, here's the list of names of the kids in the concert," Lucy set the typewritten page on the bakery work bench.

She and Hannah were decorating gingerbread men for the children participating in the Christmas Choral concert. Each cookie would have the child's name written in icing.

Hannah glanced over from where she was filling a pastry bag with royal icing.

"Christopher? Sarah-Nicole? That's going to be a tight squeeze," she grumbled good-naturedly. "I guess I'll write them vertically down the middle."

Lucy grinned. She could see the sparkle in her friend's eyes. She knew decorating gingerbread men and Christmas sugar cookies was something Hannah really enjoyed.

"I'm sure that will be fine," she commented. She looked at the bowls of assorted candies they would use for embellishments. "Hey, is that all you have for mini candy canes?"

"Mm-hmm," Hannah concentrated on her task, outlining the cookie in white icing. "Betsy keeps eating them."

Lucy chuckled. "Well, I better get more, then. I'll pop over to Red's Corner Market if that's all we need. They're closer than Bing's."

"Sounds good," Hannah murmured distractedly, piping a green bow tie on one of the boys' cookies. The girls' cookies would have red icing bows on their heads.

Lucy called out to Aunt Tricia that she'd be back in a few minutes and left through the back entrance. She drove two streets over, smiling at the sight of the new festive decorations that had popped up since the last time she'd been this way. People were even putting wreaths on their cars' front grills, and reindeer antlers decorated the roofs of a few SUVs. The town was ready for Christmas, without a doubt!

She pulled into the almost empty lot of Red's Corner Market, making a mental note to look for small containers of cotton candy, while she was here. She had an idea to use the fluffy confection for Santa's beard on a cookie order for later in the week.

As she opened the doors and stepped inside the store, she was greeted by the cheery piped in music, playing a version of "Baby, It's Cold Outside". She hummed along as she strolled through the aisles. That song had always been one of Aunt Tricia's favorites.

Adding a package of mini candy canes to her basket, Lucy wandered along, her thoughts now on Aunt Tricia. So far, no luck on the vintage ceramic tree. She'd better come up with an alternate plan, and fast. Time was running out.

Not spotting any cotton candy, she meandered a few minutes longer, then decided she'd better get back to the bakery, proceeding to the front of the store. The cashier was a young woman of about nineteen or so, standing idly by her register, scrolling through her phone. Lucy took a last look around, wondering if she was forgetting anything.

Her attention was suddenly caught by a corner display. As soon as she realized what she was seeing, her pulse began to quicken. She walked over to the small table, staring down at the goods packaged in clear cellophane wrap.

Fruitcakes, baked in fluted tube pans. Just like the poisoned fruitcake she'd seen on Taylor's desk—minus the Sweet Delights Bakery overwrap, of course. She bent to peer closely at the cakes through their packaging and felt a stirring of excitement as she spotted the green cherries. *Was this store where the killer had obtained the fruitcake for his nefarious purpose?*

She flipped over one of the cakes and recognized the label, "Pauline's Products". Not a bakery, really, more of a baking factory, she mused. Pauline's Products was a large wholesale distributor from the eastern part of the state. Still, it was quite possible that the murderer had been in this very store!

Lucy walked quickly back to the counter and cleared her throat to get the young woman's attention. The cashier pasted a smile on her face, pocketing her cellphone.

"Will that be all for you today?" She scanned the bar code of the candy cane box and looked at Lucy expectantly.

Lucy strove to keep her voice casual. "I see you have fruitcakes over there. Are they a popular item?"

The cashier shrugged. "I wouldn't say popular… it's kind of an old-fashioned thing, you know. Most of the people coming in here are after the penny candy and chocolate Santas. Oh, and perfume. We get a lot of teenagers in here trying out the perfume samples."

Lucy nodded, handing over her credit card, wondering how to get more specific information. "So, you haven't made any sales?"

The young woman swiped the card through the reader and handed it back to Lucy, shaking her head. "Oh, no, we've had a few. It's just not a best-selling item."

She bagged the box of candy canes and handed Lucy her receipt.

Lucy's mind raced as she tried to think of something to say. "Um, I was thinking of getting one for someone as a gift, but I'm not sure. Especially if they're not really popular."

The young woman nodded. "Well, I guess it all depends if the person likes fruitcake. As far as fruitcakes go, I guess they're pretty good. We've had some sales. It's just not flying off the shelves, you know." She handed Lucy her bag.

Lucy clutched the bag, unwilling to leave until she had more information. "Oh… Well, I hope the person I'm wanting to buy one for hasn't already got one! No one wants two fruitcakes, right?" She offered a smile, willing the cashier to give up a name.

The cashier grinned. "Ha! You're right. No, you're probably safe. As I said, we haven't sold too many. Although one guy has bought more than a few. He must be giving them out as gifts, I guess."

Lucy swallowed, keeping her tone casual. "Who would that be, if you don't mind me asking?"

The young woman scrunched her face up, apparently trying to recall a name. "He drives a white pickup truck with a logo on it… what's his name…"

Lucy waited, the pleasant expression on her face feeling like it was carved in stone.

The cashier pursed her lips. "It's the guy who owns the leather tannery. Do you know who I mean?"

Lucy's mouth dropped open, and she hastily shut it, croaking out a response.

"Chad Prentiss?"

The young woman nodded, smiling. "Yes! That's him! He bought five just last week."

19

Lucy walked back out to her vehicle in a daze, her mind spinning.

Could it be a coincidence that one of the suspects in Jonas's murder had purchased a fruitcake - that looked just like the poisoned fruitcake - right before the murder occurred?

She dug her phone out of her purse. She needed to let Taylor know right away.

He picked up on the second ring. "Lucy, hello."

She clutched the receiver, closing her eyes. Taylor's voice in her ear was warm and welcoming, and she heartily wished this whole case was behind them, so they could spend some quality time together. Last night had been too brief.

"Taylor... I have some news." Lucy relayed what she had found out inside Red's Market, describing the appearance of the fruitcakes, as well as the cashier's disclosure.

"I can't say for sure, of course, but I think the cakes look just like the one you found in Jonas's house. Fluted pan, green cherries. Is there any way you can test to see if the cakes are the same recipe?"

Taylor's voice sounded thoughtful. "I believe the lab could verify if the composition is the same. That's interesting, that Chad Prentiss has purchased a few."

"Interesting?" Lucy frowned. "Surely, it's not a coincidence! According to Dominic Nelson, Mr. Prentiss actually threatened Jonas with bodily harm, saying he'd shoot him if Jonas ever stepped foot on the Prentiss property again. Also, according to Lenora Nelson, Mr. Prentiss told Jonas he'd regret taking action on the matter of the polluted river water."

Taylor was silent for a beat. "Lucy, since Jonas never reported that Chad Prentiss threatened him, that doesn't leave me with much of a leg to stand on. And the results of the water test for pollutants is also still up in the air. No court action has been filed. So far, all we have is conjecture."

Lucy frowned. "Are you not going to even question Chad, then? About the fruitcakes he bought?" She couldn't help but feel disappointed. She'd thought this could be a major break in the investigation.

Taylor reassured her. "If the composition of those fruitcakes turns out to be the same as the poisoned one, then I'll have cause to investigate – and question – every person who's purchased one from Red's Market. But I need to have the cakes tested first, so we're not wasting resources on a potential dead end."

Lucy sighed. It made sense to test the cakes first. She suddenly remembered what had happened last night.

"I almost forgot to ask you. Did you question Vic D'Angelo?"

Taylor answered, his tone grim. "Yes. But as soon as I got back to the station last night, his lawyer came knocking. After that, every question I asked was answered by the lawyer, not Vic himself. I tell you, Lucy, that shady enterprise he's involved in sure does circle the wagons quickly."

Lucy's heart sank. "No results, then? Even though Vic was in Ivy Creek at the time of the murder?"

Taylor's tone was clipped. "It's such a tight-knit gang he's in, every one of them has a built-in alibi. Although we can prove Vic was in Ivy Creek, his lawyer produced a 'witness' that was supposedly in the car with him. The witness signed a statement saying they were never near Nelson Farm."

Lucy sighed. "So, unless you find another witness who spotted Vic near the farm, it's a dead end?"

"Not entirely," Taylor answered. "Since we have the gas station receipt proving he was in town when the murder occurred, combined with the fact that Vic D'Angelo has a criminal record, we were able to get a search warrant for his condo in the city. It's possible we'll find something incriminating there."

Lucy mulled that bit of info over. Although Vic D'Angelo was probably too smart to leave strychnine lying around, maybe they'd find evidence of a pre-packaged fruitcake in his condo... a discarded wrapper, or something.

She felt a glimmer of hope. Between that possibility, and the new discovery of the fruitcakes at Red's Market, she felt like maybe they'd made some progress.

"I just wish there was more I could do," she told Taylor. "I know you guys are working around the clock to solve the case, but I just feel... helpless."

"Now, Lucy. This is my job, not yours," Taylor's voice was gently chiding. "I certainly don't want you putting yourself in harm's way, trying to investigate on your own."

"Mm-hmm…" Lucy responded, trying to think of some way to help speed things along.

Taylor insisted. "Please promise me you will not seek out Chad Prentiss to question him." His tone was strict, and Lucy swallowed guiltily. She'd been thinking of doing just that.

"OK, I promise," she answered reluctantly. She was well aware of how many times Taylor had come to her rescue when she'd played amateur sleuth in the past, so she couldn't really blame him for worrying.

"Good," Taylor sighed. "I'll let you know if we find anything in Vic's condo."

They said goodbye and hung up. Lucy sat in her car, staring out the windshield at Red's Corner Market, her thoughts focused on one thing.

There had to be something she could do. The Nelson family needed justice.

20

Aunt Tricia handed the Santa Claus cupcake to the customer, smiling as the young mother passed the treat down to her delighted toddler. Within minutes, the little girl's chin was covered in frosting, but her wide grin remained even as her mother fussed, wiping at her face with a napkin. The pair made their way over to a café table to finish their treats.

"I remember when you were that age," Aunt Tricia said to Lucy, a soft expression on her face. "You loved your mother's buttercream frosting!"

Lucy grinned. "My tastes have refined," she commented. "I like the cake better than the icing now."

The bell jangled, and Betsy came in, her cheeks rosy from the cold. She smiled at the sight of the child with her messy face, before turning to Lucy and Aunt Tricia.

"I have news," she said in a low tone, coming around the counter and stashing her purse in the cubbyhole beneath it.

The three of them stepped over to the kitchen archway to speak in relative privacy.

"Joseph and I were downtown last night, having dinner at Horatio's," Betsy began.

Lucy and Aunt Tricia nodded. Although not fancy, Horatio's was a popular place for young couples on a budget to enjoy a nice meal.

"While we were there, a pair of officers came in. You'll never guess who they were after."

Lucy's eyes widened. "Who?" she whispered.

Betsy's blue eyes locked on hers. "Al Forrester!" she whispered back, checking over Lucy's shoulder to make sure her words weren't overheard. "They came in and arrested him!"

Lucy was stunned. "What?" She was confused. Taylor hadn't indicated that Al was even a strong suspect in the murder.

Aunt Tricia frowned. "Arrested him? For Jonas Nelson's murder?"

Betsy shook her head. "No, no. That's what I thought at first, but I heard the officer tell him it was for violating Heather Kelly's restraining order."

Lucy gasped, covering her mouth. "Oh, no! Is Heather OK?"

Betsy shrugged helplessly, her eyes were worried. "I don't know anything else. They just told him why he was being arrested and took him away."

Aunt Tricia laid a hand on Lucy's arm. "If Heather was hurt, Lucy, they would have arrested Al for assault."

Lucy realized her aunt was correct and relaxed somewhat. Still, whatever had happened, she felt bad for Heather. She was going through so much right now, anyway, without being harassed by her ex-husband.

"I'm going to go upstairs and call Heather," she told the two of them. "I'll be down in a few minutes."

Lucy grabbed her coffee and climbed the stairs to her office, leaving behind the chatter of a group just entering the bakery. Ivy Creek was sure seeing its share of excitement these days.

She sat behind her desk and looked up Heather's number, remembering how just a year ago Heather and Jonas had come in together to discuss their wedding cake. She knew Jonas had just been indulging Heather—he'd kept pretty quiet during the session, only speaking up to agree with Heather's choices. It saddened Lucy to know Heather wouldn't have her dream wedding.

The line rang a few times before going to voicemail. Lucy hesitated, then hung up without leaving a message. She decided she'd just drop by Heather's house. She wanted to ask Heather more about Jonas's copper wheat penny, anyway. It was possible that Heather would know if Jonas had brought it into a bank for safe keeping. That would be a possible answer to it being absent from Jonas's coin album.

Lucy retraced her steps, telling Aunt Tricia she'd been unable to reach Heather by phone. She went into the kitchen next, catching Hannah in the task of rotating trays of sugar cookies at their midpoint of baking. After Hannah assured her she was keeping up just fine with the orders, Lucy decided there was no time like the present. She'd zip over to Heather's house and be back in a flash.

Ten minutes later, she was knocking at Heather's door, waiting with bated breath. Although Aunt Tricia had made a good point, Lucy wouldn't relax until she saw for herself that Heather was unharmed.

The door opened slowly, and Heather peeked out, her face turning from wary to pleased as she spotted Lucy on her doorstep. She opened the door wide, gesturing for Lucy to come inside.

"Hey, Heather, I just wanted to check on you," Lucy admitted, relieved to see the young woman was unharmed. "I heard Al was arrested last night for violating the restraining order." She hoped Heather wouldn't feel like she was the subject of gossip.

Heather offered a quick smile and led Lucy into the living room. An orange tabby cat streaked by as they entered.

"Thanks for coming by," she began, settling herself into a chair. "Yes, I spotted Al sitting in his car outside my house yesterday, and I decided enough was enough! He's been warned to leave me alone. I finally decided to call the police and tell them I wanted to press charges for him violating the protective order."

Lucy noticed Heather looked less anxious than she had last time Lucy had seen her and privately thought Heather had made the right decision. "Oh, I'm so glad that's all there was to it," she said. "I was afraid you'd had some kind of confrontation."

Heather shook her head. "Thankfully, not."

Lucy jumped right in with her question, not wanting to take up too much of the other woman's time. "Heather, I'm not sure you've heard from Lenora Nelson, but she told me Jonas's house looked like it was ransacked a few days ago."

Heather's eyes were troubled. "Yes, I called to see how she was holding up and she told me. I'm hoping the police will find fingerprints and be able to make an arrest."

Lucy studied the young woman. "Did she tell you that Jonas's copper wheat penny was missing from its slot in the album?"

Heather nodded. "Yes, but she mentioned that maybe Jonas had hidden it somewhere else once he'd found out how valuable it was." Her hands fidgeted in her lap, twisting her engagement ring. She looked at Lucy's face. "Did she ever locate it?"

Lucy shook her head. "Not that I'm aware of." She was mildly disappointed. She'd held a glimmer of hope that Heather might have known where the coin was.

"Heather, do you think Jonas might have already sold the coin in the city?" Lucy asked. She'd had a terrible thought. What if Jonas had already sold the coin for cash, and had kept the money in his house? Maybe when the house was ransacked, the culprit had found the money.

Heather shook her head immediately. "I'm almost certain he had not," she said. "He told me he was waiting until after the New Year to get a better price. He said Christmas was not a good time to get the true value of the coin."

Lucy nodded, a little more at ease. So, it was possible that the coin would still turn up. She wondered if Taylor had made any progress with processing the scene.

Lucy stood up, giving Heather a sweet smile. "Well, I should be going. I just wanted to make sure you were OK."

Heather smiled back at her and stood up, walking Lucy to the door.

"Thanks for stopping by, Lucy. It's nice to know that someone cares."

Lucy gave her a quick hug, telling Heather to call her if she needed anything, and stepped outside. She heard Heather shut the door behind her and lock it.

As Lucy walked back to her car, she couldn't help but feel like there was something she was missing. A clue, right in front of her, that would explain everything.

She started her car and drove back to the bakery, going over every detail she knew about the case in her head, but nothing became clear.

21

Hannah set the tray of hot cinnamon rolls on the bakery workbench and removed her oven mitts. Using a rounded spatula, she liberally coated each roll with cream cheese icing, the glaze dripping off the sides onto the parchment liner.

"Did you ever manage to find that ceramic tree for Tricia?" she asked Lucy, who was busy mixing muffin batter at the next table. It was early morning, and the pair were alone in the bakery, preparing pastries before the morning rush.

Lucy added orange zest to the cranberry-walnut batter and watched as the mixer paddle swirled it in. She shook her head, looking over at her friend. "Nope. I've looked online, I've looked in thrift stores, antique shops… I guess I'll have to think of another present."

Hannah slipped on a pair of food service gloves and began transferring the rolls to a plastic tray for the front case. "Hmm. How about one of those cute stained glass bedside lamps? They make them in a bunch of styles, and I know your aunt likes to read in bed."

Lucy nodded. That wasn't a bad idea, and she needed a back-up plan. "That's a good idea, Hannah. Maybe I'll take a look on Amazon and see if there are any styles that she might like."

They heard the front door open and a moment later, Betsy came through the kitchen archway. She was wearing a pretty Christmas sweater decorated with a whimsical reindeer.

"Good morning!" she called out cheerfully. Her eyes zeroed in on the tray of cinnamon rolls. "Oooh... that would really hit the spot right about now." She glanced at Hannah. "May I?"

Hannah grinned. "Of course! After all, you are the official taste-tester."

Betsy chuckled and used the spatula to scoot a pastry onto a napkin. "And such a lovely job it is!" She nibbled on the fresh treat, heading back out front for a coffee. "Yum!"

Hannah returned the empty metal tray to the rack and peeked in the proofing closet. It was apple-cinnamon bread day, and the loaves were puffing up nicely.

"Hey, whatever happened with that creepy character that Taylor was questioning? Vic somebody..." she asked Lucy as she adjusted the temperature on the oven.

Lucy scooped some muffin batter into tulip paper liners. "Vic D'Angelo. Taylor called me last night and said they had to release him for lack of evidence. They were able to obtain a search warrant for his condo, but nothing turned up." Her tone conveyed her disappointment.

She'd really thought the police might find something that linked Vic to the poisoned fruitcake. Of course… there was always Chad Prentiss. Lucy wasn't sure which man was a more likely suspect. They both seemed unsavory characters, and both had the motive to harm Jonas. But Chad Prentiss had bought several fruitcakes at Red's, and Lucy was anxious to find out if the cake's composition matched the poisoned fruitcake from Jonas's house.

Hannah frowned. "Well, I hope they're still keeping an eye on him." She shuddered. Something about that man had gotten under her skin.

The phone rang out front and Lucy and Hannah exchanged looks. It was still a good twenty minutes before the bakery opened, but Christmas orders had been coming in at all hours. Every morning when Lucy arrived, there were at least a half-dozen messages on the voicemail, requesting call backs.

"Here we go…" Hannah intoned, and Lucy grinned.

Both were surprised to hear Betsy's worried voice next, talking on the phone.

"Uh-oh! What are you going to do?"

Lucy's hands stilled, hovering over the muffin tin. *Not more trouble*, she hoped.

A few minutes later, Betsy hung up and reappeared in the kitchen doorway.

"That was Joseph," she said with a sigh. She suddenly glanced behind herself, and they all heard the bell jangle as the front door opened.

"What happened?" asked Hannah, her eyebrows arching. "Is something wrong?"

Aunt Tricia appeared behind Betsy, bundled up against the cold. "Good morning!" She looked at Betsy, having heard Hannah's question. "What's going on?"

Betsy sighed. "Just a bump in the road, I hope. Joseph said the kids were having a choir rehearsal yesterday afternoon, and they had a visit from a few members of the school board. They just dropped in unexpectedly."

"And?" Lucy prompted.

Betsy shrugged helplessly. "He said the kids just clammed up. They were too intimidated to sing. At first, Chelsea Yeats—she sings a solo in the concert, you know—she kept singing, but when all the other kids stopped, she got too self-conscious, and eventually did, too."

"Stage fright," Lucy observed, and Betsy nodded, worried.

"Joseph tried to get them going again, but they were too nervous." She looked worried. "Now he's afraid they won't be able to perform at the concert, in front of all those people."

Aunt Tricia looked thoughtful. "You know, the only cure for stage fright is practice. Maybe Joseph needs to bring the kids out Christmas caroling a few times, just to sing in front of strangers."

"That's a good idea," Lucy said, and Betsy nodded, with a grateful look at Aunt Tricia.

"Yes, I'll mention that to him. Hopefully, it will all work out before the concert next week."

"I sure hope so," Lucy murmured. "The whole town will be there."

"It's a lot of pressure on Joseph," Betsy commented. "I really want this to go well for him."

"We'll all be there, cheering them on," said Aunt Tricia, squeezing Betsy's shoulder. "I'm sure it will go well."

Betsy brightened, smiling at the older woman.

Lucy glanced at the clock, and then out at the parking lot, which held several customers waiting in their warm cars. "We might as well open up. It looks like we already have people waiting."

She flipped the sign to "Open" and turned on the front lights. Within minutes there was a line of customers, keeping Betsy and Aunt Tricia busy in the front, while Lucy and Hannah returned to their baking in the back.

Just as the morning rush ended, Lucy's cell phone buzzed in her apron pocket. She took it out and glanced at the text message. It was Taylor, requesting she call him when she had a minute.

Telling Hannah she'd be right back, Lucy took the stairs to her office, crossing her fingers that Taylor would have some news on the case. She dialed his cell number and soon heard his familiar voice on the other end of the line.

"How are you, Lucy?" he asked. It sounded like they were busy at the police station. She could hear a lot of voices in the background.

"Pretty good," she answered. "The bakery is staying busy. Did you find any fingerprints at Jonas's house?"

"Unfortunately, no," Taylor answered. "Either the intruder wore gloves, or Jonas was a very messy person."

Lucy frowned. "That's too bad. Was that what you wanted to tell me?"

"Just a second." Taylor covered the mouthpiece for a moment and spoke to someone else. When he came back, his voice was harried. "No, I have news. I wish it was better news, but it is what it is."

Lucy held her breath, waiting.

"The fruitcakes at Red's Market do not match the composition of the poisoned fruitcake," he said without preamble. "It was a dead end."

Lucy's heart sank. "Does this mean Chad Prentiss is no longer considered a suspect?"

Taylor hesitated. "I'm not writing him off my list just yet. According to the Nelsons, he did have a verbal altercation with Jonas. And since our suspect list is pretty short, we're not giving up on Mr. Prentiss."

Lucy frowned. "Besides Vic D'Angelo and Chad Prentiss, who else is on your list?"

Taylor's answer surprised her. "Al Forrester. After we brought him in for violating the restraining order, I had a chat with him."

Lucy felt her pulse quicken. "Did he say something incriminating?"

Taylor took his time choosing his words. "Let's just say, at the present time, Mr. Forrester doesn't seem firmly grounded in reality. During my questioning of him, he repeatedly referred to Heather as his wife, and seemed confused when I pointed out they were divorced." He paused, then added. "Equally disturbing as that, he doesn't seem to recall having a chat with me a few weeks ago, when I gave him a warning to stay away from Heather."

Lucy drew in a breath. *That was pretty scary.* "What could that mean, Taylor?"

"I'm not sure," Taylor admitted. "We got a judge on board for a mandatory psychiatric evaluation before we release him. We'll see what the doctor says." There was a commotion in the background, and Lucy could hear Taylor's name being called.

"I'll let you go," she said. "Thanks for keeping me in the loop."

They said their goodbyes, and Lucy hung up the phone, pondering the fresh news.

Could Al Forrester have had some sort of psychotic break and killed Jonas in a jealous rage?

22

As Lucy descended the steps to the bakery's ground floor, she heard Betsy call her name. The young woman hurried over, speaking in a hushed tone.

"A woman called for you while you were upstairs," Betsy glanced over her shoulder as she spoke. Aunt Tricia was busy assisting a customer in buying an assortment of pastries.

"Her name was Rosalyn, from Cleo's Collectibles. She said they just acquired something you may be interested in." She continued, conspiratorially, "Hannah told me it might be about a present for Tricia, but don't worry, I didn't say a word."

Lucy brightened. *Perhaps Rosalyn had found her an Atlantic ceramic tree!*

"OK, thanks, Betsy." Lucy glanced at her watch. "I'm just going to pop out for a minute. Be back in a jiffy." Lucy hurried out the door before Aunt Tricia could finish with her customer. Although it was good of Rosalyn to alert her that she'd acquired the item, she couldn't expect the shop keeper to hold it for long, especially now, in the final days of the Christmas shopping season.

Lucy got into her SUV and zipped across town, excited by the prospect of replacing Aunt Tricia's beloved Christmas decoration. *What a lovely surprise that would be!*

Lucy was able to park right out front this time, but she still took a minute to walk over to the alley, hoping to spot the stray dog again. Unfortunately, the alley was empty. As she peered down the gloomy length of the narrow passageway, she spotted a tall, thin man at the other end, climbing a short flight of steps, before opening a door and disappearing inside the building.

She realized it must have been Rosalyn's nephew, Drew, entering the apartment in the back of the shop. It would make sense he'd have a private entrance.

She opened the door to Cleo's Collectibles a minute later and was warmly greeted by Cleo herself. The feline purred, rubbing her whiskered face on Lucy's leg.

"Hello, there, Cleo," Lucy murmured, then looked up and spotted Rosalyn, perched up on a five-foot ladder, dusting a top shelf.

"Hi, there, Rosalyn!" Lucy called out. "My assistant at the bakery said you left me a message."

Rosalyn grinned and climbed down, laying the feather duster on the ladder step, and wiping her hands on her jeans. "Hey, Lucy! Yes, look what just came in!"

The woman disappeared behind the counter, ducking down to retrieve the item.

Lucy crossed her fingers as Rosalyn popped back up with a large cardboard box and fiddled with the flaps. "I'm not sure if this is the one you're looking for," she murmured, finally reaching inside and carefully pulling out the ceramic statue.

As she withdrew the object, Lucy's hopes plummeted. Although the tree was the right height and circumference, the similarity stopped there. This tree was a light green instead of a dark forest green, and it didn't feature the snow-capped branches that Lucy had always found so charming. It was designed with the same "garland" of little Christmas lights, but Lucy could tell without Rosalyn even plugging it in, the lights were not multicolored, but clear.

Rosalyn could tell from Lucy's expression that it wasn't a match.

"Oh, well. It was worth a shot." She sighed and grinned ruefully at Lucy. "We'll keep our eyes open, but time is getting short."

Lucy nodded glumly. Although it was a little tempting to go ahead and purchase this ceramic tree, she knew if she waited long enough, she'd find one that matched Aunt Tricia's broken one. Of course, that may not happen in time for Christmas, but there would be other occasions for gift giving.

But Christmas was imminent.... Lucy glanced around. "Maybe I'll take a look around while I'm here. It looks like you have some new things in."

Rosalyn brightened, nodding her head. "Yes, Drew has been finding quite a few interesting pieces lately."

At the mention of the shopkeeper's nephew, Lucy glanced at the door behind the counter, wondering why Drew hadn't emerged yet. *It was really none of her business. Maybe he was on break or had today off.*

Lucy wandered through the aisles, admiring antique books and toys, charmed by a vintage mechanical toy elephant who lifted his trunk and trumpeted. There were scads of old vinyl albums, and Lucy flipped through them, knowing Hannah would love some of the titles.

She stepped over to another aisle and was thrilled to see an array of antique kitchenware. A vintage rotary eggbeater, a collection of whimsical egg timers, and a bunch of different character-shaped cake pans. Lucy grinned. She remembered baking her first cake in a Mickey Mouse head cake pan and decorating it with her mother's guidance.

A vintage set of nested tube pans caught her eye. *Fluted tube pans...*

Lucy lifted the set, separating them. There was a 6-inch, an 8-inch, and a 12-inch. Her brow furrowed. The most popular size was a 10-inch, and that one was missing.

"Find something you like?" asked Rosalyn from behind the counter.

Lucy glanced up and blinked as she caught a movement from behind the woman. She could swear she'd seen the door behind the counter beginning to open, but now it was closed again. *Odd.*

She glanced back down at the set of pans. "Do you have the 10-inch pan that goes with this set?" Lucy wasn't sure why she was asking, although the fact that the poisoned fruitcake had been that size flitted through her mind. *Still... 10-inch fluted tube pans could be found in practically any department store.*

Rosalyn looked puzzled. "It's not there? That's funny, I thought we had the entire set." She shrugged. "Maybe it got misplaced, or possibly Drew sold it as a separate item. I can check with him, if you'd like."

Lucy thought for a minute, then shook her head. "No, don't bother. I was just curious. I really don't need any more tube pans." She returned the set to the shelf, moving down to the end of the aisle. Nothing really seemed to jump out at her for Aunt Tricia's present.

She sighed, turning to look down the length of the long counter, spotting a glass display case. *Vintage jewelry, maybe? That may yield something interesting.*

She stepped over to the glass and was surprised to see the contents were not jewelry items at all, but coins. *Antique coins.* Her pulse quickened. She hadn't realized Rosalyn was in the business of buying and selling coins.

"Rosalyn," Lucy turned around excitedly. "Has anyone ever brought in a 1943 copper wheat penny?"

Rosalyn's eyebrows shot up. "Why, yes, but that's way out of my league. A coin like that is worth more than I could ever hope to pay for it." She looked at Lucy curiously. "Why do you ask?"

Lucy felt a mild sense of disappointment. She'd hoped maybe Rosalyn had purchased Jonas's coin, and that it hadn't been stolen, after all. "Was it Jonas Nelson who brought it in?"

Rosalyn shrugged, shaking her head. "It was a young man with dark hair. He didn't tell me his name. It was almost a month ago. I told him what it was worth and recommended he go into the city to an established coin dealer if he wanted to sell it."

Lucy pondered the woman's words. Another dead end.

Curious now, Lucy asked, "How much is a coin like that worth, anyway?"

The shopkeeper's answer stunned her.

"In mint condition, as this one was, I'd say it could be sold for up to $250,000."

23

*L*ucy's mouth dropped open. "That much?"

Rosalyn nodded. "They're very rare. They were actually minted by mistake at a time when the government had decided to use steel for pennies because of the war. The first batch that ran through were still producing copper, but the mistake was caught, resulting in a very limited number cast in copper that year."

Lucy felt a sudden conviction. This *must* have been the reason that Jonas was murdered. Not jealousy, not a dispute over polluted water. Someone had killed him for this very valuable coin. *Was it possible that Vic D'Angelo knew about the coin?*

Her musings were suddenly interrupted by the buzzing of her cell phone - a text message. Pulling her phone from her bag, Lucy read the message from Hannah.

Can you pick up molasses? Just got another gingerbread order.

Lucy typed in *Yes* and turned back to Rosalyn. "I've got to be going. Thanks for letting me know about the tree. I'm sorry I won't be purchasing it."

Rosalyn waved away her apology. "I'll keep my eye out. Maybe another one will come in."

Lucy thanked her and exited the shop, her mind still reeling from the knowledge of the coin's worth. Definitely something to share with Taylor, she thought.

After a quick stop at Bing's, Lucy headed on back to the bakery. She joined Hannah, and together they baked and decorated, fulfilling the many orders that had come in. Finally, at five-thirty that evening they were caught up, and parted ways.

Lucy saw Hannah stifle a yawn as she unlocked her car, waving goodbye as Lucy pulled out of the parking lot. Lucy was feeling the long day and decided when she got home, she'd reward herself with a nice bubble bath. Tomorrow would be another long day.

As she drove through the pretty neighborhood, lit up with red and green twinkling lights, her phone rang. Unwilling to glance at the caller ID while driving, she clicked the button, answering in her best professional voice.

"Lucy Hale, how may I help you?"

An unfamiliar voice greeted her. "Is this Lucy who's looking for the Atlantic ceramic tree?"

Lucy frowned, but before she could answer, the man hurried on to say, "This is Drew Sykes, of Cleo's Collectibles. I stumbled upon one of your trees this afternoon, in mint condition! Thought I'd give you a call."

Lucy grinned, her spirits buoyed by the good news. "That's great! Can you describe it?"

Drew went on to describe the dark green color, snow-capped branches, and multi-colored twinkling lights. "Just like you had requested in our notes," he finished. "But I have another party interested that will be coming in tomorrow. Could you come by now?"

Lucy's brow furrowed, and she glanced at the clock on the dashboard. "I don't know if I can get there before you close. Don't you close at six?"

"I can wait a few minutes," he offered. "As long as we can wrap it up by six-thirty."

Lucy hesitated a minute, then decided to go for it. The shop wasn't that far away, and it would be such a relief to have Aunt Tricia's present all taken care of!

"Sure," she answered, pulling into a driveway to turn around. "I'll be there shortly."

On her journey across town, she passed the theater, just a few streets over from Cleo's Collectibles. Joseph and Miles were herding a large group of children down the sidewalk, all of whom carried songbooks.

With a grin, she realized Joseph had taken Aunt Tricia's suggestion to heart, and was bringing the children out caroling, door to door, to cure them of their stage fright. If she hadn't been pressed for time she would have stopped and joined them–she adored caroling, though it had been many years. She tooted her horn and waved, seeing Joseph raise a hand in return.

The shutters were closed on the storefront windows as Lucy parked out front, and she had a moment of panic–had Drew not waited for her? But as she approached the front steps, the door to the shop opened, and Drew appeared, ushering her inside.

"Thank you so much for letting me have first dibs on the tree," Lucy said. "I've looked everywhere, with no luck."

"It can be rather difficult to find such a specific model on short notice," Drew said as they walked together to the front counter. "Fortunately, I have a connection in the city and I was able to put the word out."

Lucy looked around, expecting to see Rosalyn and Cleo. "Have Rosalyn and Cleo left for the day?" She'd assumed Cleo lived in the shop, but it made more sense that she lived with Rosalyn at her house.

"Yes… yes, they have…" Drew seemed distracted, looking back toward the street.

Lucy glanced down the length of the front counter, expecting to see the ceramic tree. "So, the tree…"

Drew walked behind the counter and opened the door that led to his apartment. He beckoned to Lucy.

"I just got back before I called you. I brought it in the back and haven't yet unboxed it. C'mon back here."

He disappeared into the apartment, and Lucy stared after him for a moment, confused. *Hadn't she seen him return hours ago? Maybe he'd gone back out, and that's when he'd found it.*

Drew popped his head back through the doorway, looking mildly annoyed. "Ms. Hale?"

Lucy tried to calm the nervous jitters suddenly plaguing her. Drew Sykes had done her a favor, staying behind after closing, and here she was, irritating him. She tamped down her lingering uneasiness and followed him through the doorway.

Lucy looked around the small apartment, finding herself in a combination kitchen/living room area. The space was dimly lit, and the shades were all drawn. Her eyes skittered over the messy kitchen, dirty dishes and pans lining the counter. Obviously, Drew liked to cook, but cleaning up was not his forte. She hurriedly looked away before she offended him with her nosiness.

There was a door at the back of the large room, an alternate entrance which Lucy assumed was the one that opened into the alley. Drew hefted a large cardboard box onto the coffee table and undid the flaps. He motioned for her to join him.

"I don't want to go to the trouble of unpacking it if it's the wrong one," he said. "I've got Styrofoam wedges in there, placed just so. Maybe you should verify the color first."

Lucy walked over and peered down inside the box. There was a ceramic tree in there, alright, but if she wasn't mistaken, it was the light green one Rosalyn had already shown her. She looked up with a frown.

"But I thought…"

Her words died, unspoken, as she saw Drew looming above her, his face twisted with malice as he brought a brass bookend crashing down upon her head.

24

There was a ringing in her ears when Lucy opened her eyes. The light stabbed her pupils with excruciating pain, and she hurriedly squeezed them shut again, trying to remember what had happened. The crown of her head throbbed in time to her heartbeat, and she felt slightly sick to her stomach. *Had she been in an accident?*

The sound of water running caused her to frown, and she peeked through slitted eyelids, seeing an unfamiliar man standing in front of a sink, his back to her.

As her wavering vision took in the messy countertops stacked with dishes, it suddenly all came rushing back.

Drew Sykes had attacked her! What was he planning to do?

Lucy opened her mouth to scream and found, to her horror, she had been gagged. A tug at her wrists when she moved her arms filled her with the knowledge he'd bound her hands to the chair she was sitting in. She wiggled her feet next, offering a silent prayer of gratitude as she realized he had not tied her feet. *She just needed to get her hands free.*

Trying to ignore the pain in her head, Lucy watched Drew warily while she frantically tried to stretch the knots at her wrists. Standing with his back to her, she couldn't tell what he was doing. Mixing something, maybe?

Her eyes roamed over the cluttered countertops, and she suddenly gasped, her hands stilling.

There was a 10-inch fluted tube pan, crusty with residue.

Drew must have heard Lucy's indrawn breath because he spun around at once, catching Lucy's gaze riveted on the dirty baking pan.

"Ah, yes, I can see that you've figured it out," he said, sounding strangely pleased. He walked slowly toward her, and Lucy's heart hammered with terror.

Drew Sykes had killed Jonas! Was he going to kill her as well?

"I thought you were getting close to the truth when I heard you talking to my aunt about copper wheat pennies."

He stopped in front of her, looking amused. "I must admit, Ms. Hale, you made my job much easier with the popularity of your fruitcakes." His voice was a sneer. "All I had to do was buy one at Bing's Grocery and use your bakery packaging to wrap my own 'special' concoction."

His eyes crinkled with mad humor. "No one can say no to a Sweet Delights Bakery fruitcake, right? I just picked the flimsy lock on Jonas's front door and left the cake as a present on his kitchen counter." Drew chuckled at the memory.

"No doubt he thought one of the doting females in his life had dropped it off. No questions asked, just... bam! Dead as a doornail." His lips pursed, considering. "It's really too bad he didn't share some with that stupid dog of his. I was able to bribe the mutt with hamburger while I went about my business there, but now the blasted creature has followed me here. Almost like it knows I was responsible for its master's death."

Drew frowned at the thought, but then shook his head. "No matter, now. I have some special holiday brew mixed up for you, Lucy Hale, and I'm sure there will be enough left over for the pooch." He held up a soda bottle with a fizzy, clear liquid inside.

At Lucy's look of horror, he snickered. "A little strychnine sparkling tonic, to make all your holiday troubles disappear."

Lucy shrunk away from him, pressing back into the chair with terror in her heart. *He was going to make her drink poison!*

Drew leaned menacingly close, his eyes boring into her own. "But first... I don't suppose you know where Jonas stashed that coin, do you?" He narrowed his eyes as Lucy shook her head, her eyes wide as her mind raced. *She had to get free!*

"Hmm. I really didn't think you did, but it was worth a shot. I'll just have to go back and do another search. No one will be watching his house too closely, not after your dead body turns up at the leather tannery. They'll be busy locking up Chad Prentiss on a double murder charge."

As Lucy blinked in surprise, Drew nodded smugly. "Men talk, Lucy. Pour a beer into any of the local yokels in this town and they'll tell you all about their troubles. Chad Prentiss was only too happy to complain about his little beef with Jonas. That's how I came upon my idea in the first place. After Jonas came in here with his coin, I could tell he didn't deserve that kind of treasure; a fortune, right there in his palm."

He looked irritated, thinking back. "I'm not sure why my aunt felt like she had to be straight with him. A little wheeling and dealing, and that coin would have been ours! In this life, you need to take what you want with both hands, or you'll never rise to the top." He sighed, shaking his head. "That farm boy, straight off the hay wagon. He told my aunt he kept that beauty in a coin album… like an eleven-year-old child would!" He snorted.

Straightening up, he lifted the bottle of sinister liquid up to the light, examining the contents. "Well, time's a-wasting. Might as well get it done, don't you think?"

Lucy's eyes bugged out as Drew reached out a hand toward her head. "We can do this easy, or hard," he said, his tone a warning. "But either way, you're going to drink it."

Lucy struggled violently, rocking back and forth and side to side, but Drew managed to grab her by the hair. The sore spot on her scalp had her crying out in pain and abruptly ceasing her efforts to evade him.

"Relax. It'll be over before you know it," he promised, and Lucy shut her eyes in despair, a solitary tear leaking out.

Suddenly, there was a heavy pounding upon the antique shop's front door.

25

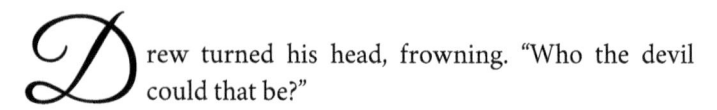

$\mathcal{D}$rew turned his head, frowning. "Who the devil could that be?"

The heavy knocking repeated, and he turned to scowl at Lucy. "Who knows you're here?"

Lucy shook her head, wide-eyed, as Drew set down the bottle and picked up the brass bookend from the floor. He cracked open the door leading to the antique shop, peering out. Lucy prayed it wasn't Hannah or Betsy out there, alone. She had no idea how much time had passed or if anyone was even looking for her.

She redoubled her efforts, working on stretching the knots, and felt a slackness in the bindings around her wrists, filling her with hope. Drew slipped silently out the apartment door, sidling over to the shop window, apparently trying to see who was on the front steps.

Lucy concentrated, trying to slip her wrists through the loop of rope holding her to the chair. *She needed to get loose before he returned!*

Success! One wrist slipped through the loop and Lucy twisted in the chair, reaching behind herself, yanking at the thin rope still wrapped around her other hand.

Just as she managed to free herself, an ethereal sound began to echo through the antique store. Faint strains of music floated in the air, drifting into the apartment. Lucy ripped the gag from her mouth, breathing heavily from her exertions, and tried to identify the sound.

A group of children were sweetly singing, "O Holy Night", like a choir of angels.

It was Joseph, and Miles, and the kids, out caroling door to door!

Lucy froze, free of her bindings. She crouched over the chair, debating her choices. She could call for help and hope Joseph would hear her, but she ran the risk of Drew returning and knocking her out… or worse.

She spied the door leading to the alley and bolted for it, praying it wasn't locked with a key. She flipped the simple latch bolt, and tugged the doorknob, filled with gratitude when it opened without issue.

Lucy fled through the door into the twilight outside, stumbling down the steps and racing headlong through the alley, the pain in her head growing worse by the minute.

"Help! Somebody, please! Help me!" Her voice was hoarse with emotion, and she feared no one would hear her. Her limbs tingled with a strange sensation, and she didn't feel quite in control of her movements. She stumbled over an unseen object and almost lost her balance, arms flailing.

Suddenly, she heard a bellow of rage from behind her, and the unmistakable sound of a door slamming. Casting a fearful look over her shoulder, she saw Drew racing after her, his long legs closing the distance between them too fast.

"Get back here! You're only going to make this worse for yourself!"

With rubbery legs, Lucy ran on, wondering what he would do if he caught her. *What could be worse than being poisoned?* She knew she didn't want to find out.

"Help me! Police!" she yelled, just as her foot got tangled in some debris, causing her to lose her balance. She stumbled sideways, trying to regain her footing before it was too late, but careened forward, stretching out her hands to break her fall.

"Oof..." Lucy went down hard, landing on her front.

The wind was knocked out of her, causing her to lay gasping like a fish, unable to draw oxygen into her starving lungs. Her mind commanded her body to get up and run, but she felt paralyzed, unable to do anything but try to breathe.

"You're gonna regret this..." Drew's menacing words came from right behind her, and Lucy squeezed her eyes shut, more terrified than she'd ever been in her life.

She opened her mouth, willing herself to yell, to move, to do something, but her chest heaved silently as her body labored to breathe.

Suddenly, she heard a snarl, and a scrambling of paws racing on asphalt. A dark form in shadow whooshed by her, and she heard Drew's bellow of alarm.

"Get away! Go! Aaaah!" He cried out in pain and Lucy could hear the sounds of a vicious animal attack. Snarling and tearing, screams of pain and terror filled the alleyway.

Lucy focused on crawling forward, unable to get up and run. Her head felt like it had been split in two. She dragged herself forward a few feet, then a few feet more, leaving Drew and the attacking animal behind her. Her legs still refused to move, and she wondered if it was a result of her head injury.

She couldn't crawl anymore. Her skull hurt too much. The sidewalk, illuminated by a streetlamp, was only ten feet away, but it could have been a mile. She could still hear the choir of children singing. Lucy lay there, waiting, gathering her strength, knowing she couldn't compete with their voices. Her vision began to waver, graying on the edges.

As the carol came to a close, the children's voices ebbed away. Lucy took a deep breath and yelled with all the strength she had left.

"Help me! In the alley! Help! Help!"

The stabbing pain in her head from her efforts caused her to see stars, and Lucy closed her eyes, praying someone would come before Drew got to her.

Hurried footfalls came from the direction of the street, and Lucy opened her eyes, seeing the silhouette of a man a few feet away, on the sidewalk.

"Oh my God! Lucy!"

It was Joseph. He rushed forward and kneeled down beside her. She whispered, "Call 911. Drew Sykes. Killer."

Blackness washed over her world, then, taking all her senses with it.

Lucy passed out.

26

Chelsea Yeats's voice sounded pure and sweet as she performed her solo without a hitch. Enthusiastic applause sounded all around the auditorium, and the little girl blushed with pleasure, stepping back to join the rest of the choir in their rendition of "Silent Night".

As the final notes echoed and faded away, the crowd exploded, whistling, stamping their feet, clapping and cheering. The children bowed as a group, with Joseph standing proudly by.

He stepped to the microphone, addressing the audience.

"Thank you so much! We'll have a short intermission. There are refreshments to be had in the lobby."

Lucy, Taylor, Betsy, Hannah, and Aunt Tricia rose from their seats, following the throng of people out to the lobby.

"That was fantastic!" Betsy's eyes were shining with delight. "Not a bit of stage fright left."

"Joseph taking the children out caroling might have saved the concert," Hannah observed. She glanced around the large lobby, and Lucy guessed she was hoping to spot Miles in the crowd.

"Well, it certainly saved me," Lucy commented. "In the literal sense."

Lucy didn't remember much of what happened after Joseph had found her in the alley. She'd drifted in and out of consciousness, all the way to the hospital in an ambulance. Joseph had supplied the details when she'd awoken in the hospital bed, with her head bandaged up from the nasty blow Drew had dealt her, and her family and friends gathered around.

When the police had arrived, they'd discovered Ivan, the Nelson's dog, had apprehended Drew. Drew was badly mauled and lay bleeding on the ground, with Ivan determinedly guarding him. Drew was terrified and begged the police to take him to a hospital.

Drew gave a full confession in the presence of two officers, knowing that Lucy would be alerting them the moment she regained consciousness. He'd thought by confessing he might get a lighter sentence. Taylor had later ensured that did not happen, and Drew Sykes was now facing charges for murder and attempted murder.

Lucy had come away with a concussion, resulting in an overnight stay at the hospital. She was grateful that the temporary paralysis she'd experienced was gone by the time she awoke. The doctor explained that the nerves throughout the body could be affected by such a daunting blow to the head.

Taylor squeezed her hand now, his look one of gentle concern. "How are you feeling? Too much sound?"

Lucy shook her head. It had been three days since the incident had occurred, and she'd been very sensitive to light and sound for the first forty-eight hours. But she was feeling fine now, and she smiled at Taylor, squeezing his hand in return.

"I'm fine. Just a little tired." She looked around and spotted Heather Kelly. "Hey, Heather!"

The young woman was dressed in a sparkling red sweater and a long plaid skirt. She waved and headed over to their group. Lucy knew Taylor had filled the woman in on all that had happened.

"Hi, guys! What a great concert!" She looked at Lucy solicitously. "How are you feeling, Lucy?"

Lucy smiled, responding, "I'm doing fine, thanks. I heard you helped find Jonas's copper wheat penny!"

Heather chuckled. "Pure luck! As soon as I found out what had happened, with Ivan attacking that man, I remembered Jonas had brought over a manila envelope with Ivan's vet records and rabies tags in it. He said he kept misplacing it, so he left it in my desk. I thought the police would need verification that Ivan was up to date on his vaccinations, since he'd bitten someone. Imagine my surprise when I peeked in there and found that coin!"

"That dog is a hero," commented Aunt Tricia. "If he hadn't attacked that awful man, who knows what would have happened."

Heather nodded. "He is such a good dog. I'm so glad he's been brought home to Lenora."

She looked around at their group. "Well, I might as well tell you all now. I've decided to move out to the east coast and make a fresh start."

There were murmurs of surprise, and Heather continued with a rueful smile. "I just need to get away from all the memories. I still see Jonas everywhere I look. My sister lives in New Hampshire, so I thought I'd try it there for a while."

Lucy nodded sympathetically. "I totally understand, but I hate to see you go."

"When are you moving?" Hannah asked.

Heather replied, "Right after the New Year. I've found someone to rent my house until I decide what to do with it. He's an animal lover, and he was quite enamored of my fenced-in yard. He said he takes in stray dogs as a foster parent until they can be placed with forever homes."

Betsy smiled. "That's so sweet! Is he new to town?"

Heather nodded. "Yes, just moved here from Illinois. You've probably already met him, Betsy, seeing that he works for Joseph now."

Lucy looked at Hannah and grinned as Betsy replied, "Oh! You must mean Miles. Yeah... he seems like such a sweet guy."

Hannah blushed as Lucy nudged her, but neither Betsy nor Heather seemed to notice.

Heather glanced at her watch. "Well, I need to get some hot chocolate before intermission is over. I'm so glad you're OK, Lucy. Merry Christmas, everyone! I'm sure I'll stop in at the bakery before I leave town."

The group echoed back with "Merry Christmas!" Waving cheerily at them all, Heather headed toward the refreshment stand.

Aunt Tricia looked at Lucy's wide grin and Hannah's pink cheeks. "What did I miss?"

Lucy shook her head, her eyes sparkling. "Nothing."

The lights flicked on and off three times in succession, indicating intermission was about to end, so the group moved toward the double doors to the auditorium, eagerly anticipating more choral delights.

As they seated themselves, shoulder to shoulder, waiting for the lights to dim, Lucy counted her blessings.

Her life had been spared. Nelson Farm would be saved. Ivan was back home, safe and sound. Jonas's killer had been brought to justice. And maybe... just maybe, Hannah would find romance in the New Year.

Lucy snuggled against Taylor's arm around her shoulder, thankful for the Christmas miracles bestowed upon Ivy Creek.

GIGI PEERED out from between the branches of the evergreen, allowing herself to be rescued by Lucy. After lifting her free of the branches, Lucy brushed off the tinsel that had stuck to the cat's fluffy white fur, scolding her indulgently.

"You know you don't like it once you've climbed in there, so why do you keep doing it?"

She set the feline on the carpet, and Gigi flounced away with a flick of her tail.

Lucy sighed, shaking her head with a smile, as Aunt Tricia chuckled.

"You know, maybe we should get a smaller tree next year. This one is just too tempting for her. A forest, just waiting to be explored."

Lucy responded with good humor, "A smaller tree might topple from her weight. She's gained a pound this year, you know." She bent to retrieve a large box from under the tree, dragging it over to set it before her aunt.

"Oh, my, what's this?" Aunt Tricia peered down at the gaily wrapped box, teasing Lucy. "It's big enough to be a new car!"

"And what would you do with a new car?" Lucy countered with a smile. "You're so attached to that old sedan of yours."

Aunt Tricia looked at Lucy over her spectacles, as she began to tear the wrapping paper off the plain brown box. "Now, you know, there are too many memories in that old car for me to ever get rid of it."

She continued speaking as she opened the criss-crossed cardboard flaps. "I remember, your uncle used to drive us all the way to…"

Her words died as she peered inside the box and saw her gift.

"Oh, my goodness, Lucy! Wherever did you find one?" Aunt Tricia's eyes sparkled with delight.

"I had a little help from Taylor." Lucy grinned and assisted her aunt, lifting the Atlantic ceramic tree from the box, and placing it before her on the carpet. It was a bit of luck that a fellow officer in Taylor's squad was in possession of the vintage decoration, and willing to part with it.

The tree stood twenty-two inches tall and was an exact replica of the one that her uncle had given Aunt Tricia so many years ago. Lucy reached for the nearby extension cord and plugged the tree in, watching her aunt's face as the lights began to twinkle on and off.

Aunt Tricia's face glowed with joy as she looked at the sight.

"Oh, my dear… it's so beautiful! Just like the one your uncle gave to me."

She pulled Lucy into a fond embrace, and the two of them sat watching the twinkling lights, each lost in their own memories of Christmases long ago.

A merry Christmas it was, indeed.

The End

LENORA NELSON'S DOG BISCUITS

INGREDIENTS:

- 2 1/4 tsp dry yeast
- 1/4 cup warm water
- 4 cups beef broth
- 3 1/2 cups all-purpose flour
- 2 cups whole wheat flour
- 1 cup stone-ground cornmeal
- 1 cup rye flour
- 1/3 cup non-fat dry milk
- 4 tsp wheat germ

PROCEDURE:

Add yeast to water, stir and let sit for 10 minutes.

Whisk together all the dry ingredients in a large bowl.

Add the beef broth to the yeast mixture, and then pour the combination over the dry ingredients, mixing as much as you can by hand.

See if the dough will stick together if compressed in your fist. If not, add a little more liquid.

Turn out half the dough at a time onto a floured surface, knead until smooth. Cover the unused dough with a damp tea towel so it doesn't dry out.

Roll the dough out in batches, into sections about 1/4 inch thick. Cut into 4" x 2" rectangles or use a dog bone shaped cutter. You may re-roll scraps, but you might need to add a little water or broth.

Preheat the oven to 300 degrees F, and line your baking pans with tin foil.

Bake the dog cookies for 45 minutes to 1 hour, until browned and firm when pressed on the center.

Cool completely and store in an airtight container for 1 month or freeze for up to 6 months. Re-crisp thawed biscuits in a 400 F oven for 10 minutes.

Yields approx. 5 dozen, depending on size of cutter

AFTERWORD

Thank you for reading ***Deadly Bites on Winter Nights***. I really hope you enjoyed reading it as much as I had writing it!

If you have a minute, please consider leaving a review on Amazon or the retailer where you got it.

Many thanks in advance for your support!

A JUICY STEAK TRAGEDY

CHAPTER 1 SNEAK PEEK

CHAPTER 1 SNEAK PEEK

*K*ey in hand, Lucy paused for a moment outside Sweet Delights Bakery to admire the front window display she and her crew had finished yesterday. Valentine's Day was right around the corner, and the shop was all decked out for the occasion.

A mockup of a three-tiered wedding cake took center stage, surrounded by white gauzy tulle and pearl strands. Heart-shaped balloons floated on glitzy ribbons, rising from behind a small table adorned with a ruffled tablecloth in pink. A silver platter set on top was stacked with Valentine's Day cookies—heart shaped and sporting sentimental messages. Tiny paper hearts and confetti dotted the red silk fabric they'd used as the floor covering.

Lucy smiled as she unlocked the front door and flipped on the lights. Valentine's Day was one of her favorite holidays in the bakery, both because she found the red and pink color scheme cheery in the midst of winter–and the fact that chocolate was the signature sweet. How could you go wrong with chocolate?

As Lucy stepped inside, she noticed someone had pushed a flyer under the door while they were closed. She picked it up and studied it curiously. The bell jangled at her shoulder as Hannah, her number one employee, let herself in.

"Brrrr!" Hannah rubbed her mittened hands together. "A good day to work in front of the ovens!" She peered at the flyer Lucy held. "What's that?"

Lucy read the bold type at the top. "It's advertising that new restaurant that opened a few weeks ago - Sizzle." She glanced at Hannah, "Been there yet?"

Hannah shook her head. "I've been sticking close to home, but my Mom and Dad went the first week it opened, and they raved about the flavor of their steak and chicken. I guess Sizzle's got a kickin' marinade!"

Lucy cocked an eyebrow. "Better than Wrigley's?"

Wrigley's Steakhouse was an Ivy Creek icon that had been around for decades. Wrigley's claim to fame was their family marinade recipe that had been passed down through three generations. It was a closely guarded secret, one that Lionel Wrigley, the owner, refused to share – even when interviewed by a popular foodie magazine last year.

Hannah nodded, as she scanned the advertised specials on the flyer. "According to my mom, yes." She looked at Lucy. "Looks yummy! You should get Taylor to take you for Valentine's Day."

The two turned as the door opened again.

"Hello, hello," Betsy came breezing in, her cheeks pink from the cold, and her eyes sparkling. "What a lovely morning!"

Lucy's youngest employee had a glow about her, as she'd had almost continuously for the past six months that she'd been dating Joseph Hiller, Ivy Creek's local theater director. The two were almost inseparable, and Lucy suspected there would be wedding bells within the next year.

"Good morning," Lucy held the flyer up for Betsy to see. "Have you guys been to Sizzle yet? They have some great appetizers and entrees listed."

Betsy hung up her coat and retrieved her apron from behind the counter. She shook her head.

"We've been working around the clock on this production," she said. "I'm so glad I volunteered to help backstage. Just the costuming alone is so intense and don't even get me started on the scenery! Thank goodness we have a bunch of college kids helping out."

The Ivy Creek Theater was putting on a production of Romeo and Juliet, just in time for Valentine's Day. The whole town was buzzing about it.

"Isn't opening night tonight?" asked Hannah, pouring herself a cup of coffee.

Betsy grinned and nodded. "It is! You guys should come."

Lucy shook her head as she set up the cappuccino machine. "I promised Aunt Tricia we'd go together, and she has her book club tonight. But we're planning to come, soon."

Betsy nodded, though she looked disappointed. "Hannah? How about you? If you don't want to sit by yourself in the audience, you can come watch from backstage with me. It'll be fun!"

Hannah busied herself with a notepad, taking stock of what pastries needed to be baked today. "Hmm. Probably not, but thanks."

Betsy cast a puzzled look at Lucy, who shrugged. Although Lucy had her own theory why Hannah didn't want to go, it wasn't her place to bring it up.

"OK," Betsy said. "Let me know if you change your mind." She looked at the clock. "Isn't Tricia working today?" Lucy's Aunt Tricia was never late, and it was almost time to open the doors.

Lucy nodded. "She stopped at the bank first. She should be here any minute." As she said the words, Aunt Tricia's blue sedan pulled into the parking lot. "Oh, there she is!"

"Oh, good." Betsy ducked down behind the counter for a minute, then popped back up. "I'm just going to go get another roll of register tape. Be right back."

She headed for the staircase to the upper level, where Lucy's office and the stockroom were located, along with a large veranda for dining in the warm weather.

When Betsy was out of earshot, Lucy approached Hannah. "You can come to the play with me and Aunt Tricia, you know. I'm not even sure if Taylor's going to come. It could be a girls' night out."

Hannah offered a small smile. "Maybe. Thanks."

Lucy studied her friend, not sure if she was overstepping. "Hannah, I hope you're not going to avoid the theater forever because of…" Lucy stopped speaking as Hannah's eyes widened.

"Miles," Hannah whispered. She looked alarmed.

Lucy frowned. "Yes. That's what I was going to say. Just because Miles didn't accept your invitation on New Year's Eve–"

"No!" Hannah hissed. "He's here! Miles is here!" She jutted her chin at the front window overlooking the parking lot.

Lucy turned and saw Aunt Tricia walking across the parking lot chatting with Miles Clifton, Joseph's new assistant. Hannah had met Miles a few months ago, and Lucy had seen instantly that her friend had a crush on the strapping, red-haired man. Especially once they'd found out Miles was actively involved with animal rescue, fostering stray dogs until they found forever homes. Hannah was known to have a giant soft spot when it came to animals.

At Lucy's urging, Hannah had invited Miles out for a drink on New Year's Eve. Lucy had been quite surprised to hear from Hannah that Miles had politely declined. Shy already, Hannah was mortified at the turn of events and had been avoiding the theater ever since.

"Hannah..." Lucy turned back, but Hannah had gone, disappearing into the kitchen.

The bell jangled, and Aunt Tricia preceded Miles into the bakery.

"Look who I found, out in the freezing weather, without even a hat or gloves!" Aunt Tricia bustled in behind the counter, dropping her purse and snagging two coffee cups.

"Black, or cream and sugar?" she asked Miles, picking up the coffeepot.

He smiled, showing straight, and even, white teeth. "Black, please," he said.

He looked to Lucy, next, with a friendly expression. "Hi, Lucy. How goes it?" His eyes met hers, then flickered away, roaming around the bakery.

"I'm good!" Lucy smiled. "Are you all ready for opening night?"

His green eyes twinkled as he responded her with good humor. "As ready as we're going to be."

Once again, Miles glanced around, peering over Lucy's shoulder in the direction of the kitchen.

"Is Hannah around?"

A JUICY STEAK TRAGEDY

AN IVY CREEK COZY MYSTERY

RUTH BAKER

ALSO BY RUTH BAKER

The Ivy Creek Cozy Mystery Series

Which Pie Goes with Murder? (Book 1)

Twinkle, Twinkle, Deadly Sprinkles (Book 2)

Waffles and Scuffles (Book 3)

Silent Night, Unholy Bites (Book 4)

Waffles and Scuffles (Book 5)

Cookie Dough and Bruised Egos (Book 6)

A Sticky Toffee Catastrophe (Book 7)

Dough Shall Not Murder (Book 8)

Deadly Bites on Winter Nights (Book 9)

A Juicy Steak Tragedy (Book 10)

NEWSLETTER SIGNUP

Want **FREE** COPIES OF FUTURE **CLEANTALES** BOOKS, FIRST NOTIFICATION OF NEW RELEASES, CONTESTS AND GIVEAWAYS?

GO TO THE LINK BELOW TO SIGN UP TO THE NEWSLETTER!

https://cleantales.com/newsletter/